“WHEN YOU SAID YOU NEEDED YOUR SPACE, I DIDN'T EXPECT YOU TO GO OUT AND FILL IT WITH ANOTHER MAN.”

“I didn't plan it! It . . . it just happened.” Carol realized that she had hurt Sean, could see the pain etched into the craggy lines of his handsome face. “Stop looking at me like that. I didn't do anything wrong!”

“Who are you trying to convince? Me . . . or yourself?” He laughed bitterly. “I can see the guilt in your eyes.”

Sean had never treated her this way before. His anger made her realize that she could lose him forever—as a friend and as a lover—and she didn't think she could bear that. “What else do you see in my eyes?” she whispered.

“The same thing that frightens you in mine,” he murmured huskily. Sean could no longer help himself. He wrapped his arms around her, reveling in the feel of her body so close to his.

Carol didn't struggle. His arms felt too good around her. She tilted her head to look up at him, knowing what he was about to do and wanting it to happen. It had been only days since their last kiss, but it seemed like years. Suddenly the only thing Carol wanted was to forget the confusion and pain and make up for lost time. . . .

Moonlight and Mistletoe

Linda Vail

A DELL BOOK

Published by
Dell Publishing
a division of
Bantam Doubleday Dell Publishing Group, Inc.
666 Fifth Avenue
New York, New York 10103

ISBN: 0-440-20474-7

Printed in the United States of America

Published simultaneously in Canada

December 1989

10 9 8 7 6 5 4 3 2 1

KRI

A WONDERFUL FACT TO REFLECT UPON, THAT EVERY HUMAN CREATURE IS CONSTITUTED TO BE THAT PROFOUND SECRET AND MYSTERY TO EVERY OTHER.

—*Charles Dickens*

1

"Oh, Carol! He's positively gorgeous! And so big!"

"He is rather well endowed, isn't he?" Carol Applegate bent to study the masculine part in question, touching it lightly with the sharp edge of her chisel. "Maybe I should trim a bit off. You think?"

Her assistant gasped. "Don't you dare!"

"Honestly, Bobbi. It's supposed to be part of your job to temper my artistic flights of fancy with a calm, detached opinion. He's just a hunk of marble."

"He's a hunk all right," the other woman agreed with a heartfelt sigh. Eyes agleam, she ran her fingertips along the statue's smooth, manly contours. Although made of stone and in quarter scale, the lifelike naked form filled her mind with wicked thoughts. "God! You're a wizard with chest muscles. Legs too. And those buns! If my husband looked like this I'd—"

"Bobbi!" Carol interrupted, laughing. "Get a grip!"

"I'd love to."

Carol batted her hand away. "Stop fondling

the merchandise. We're running low on kitsch, so we have to pour some of those pesky bronze lions this morning. Go fire up the melting pot for me, please." She eyed the spots of high color on Bobbi's cheekbones. "I daresay you won't need a match to light the burner, as overheated as you are."

"Sorry. But you know I'm always this way at Christmas for some reason." She gave the statue a final pat on the buttocks. "David turns sentimental, our kids start climbing the walls, and I get horny."

"Hornier, you mean," Carol corrected, pointedly covering the miniature naked gladiator on her workbench with a sheet. "I imagine David's glad you came to work for me; from what you've told me of your sex life, the poor man needs the rest. Are you sure you're only five years younger than I am?"

"Thirty-two is closer to a woman's supposed sexual peak than twenty-seven, so by that yardstick you should be the randy one. It's not my age, it's all the excitement. 'Tis the season for love, I suppose."

"Humbug!"

Bobbi stepped over to the wall opposite the workbench, where a row of hooks held various protective garments. She chose a leather apron and gloves for each of them, as well as two full-face shields with flip-up visors, then carried them across the studio to the metal casting area. There, she fired up the foundry's gas burner. It came to life with a *wooshing* roar, loud enough so that she had to raise her voice to be heard.

"Humbug?" she asked. "Come on, Carol. You've been pretty excited yourself since that Richard Palance guy came to town. And don't tell me it's only because he commissioned you to make that . . . that bizarre *thing* for presentation to the American Ski Team."

"That *thing* is a very lucrative project. You know, as in money? The stuff that keeps me in business and pays your salary? And it is not bizarre," Carol added. "It's what we sculptors refer to as avant-garde."

"Well, I'm just your average menial, and I say it looks like a ball of barbed wire with feet."

"Enough!" Carol started tidying her workbench, an act of habit that also allowed her to hide the smile that said she agreed with her employee's critical assessment. "You know it's Richard's own design, and he has a very sensitive ego."

After making sure the bench was as neat and clean as everything else around her, Carol went to join Bobbi at the foundry. It was already much warmer in this corner of the converted two-car garage that served as her studio, would be hotter still when the cast-iron crucible came up to operating temperature. They would soon be sweating in spite of a big overhead exhaust fan and the cold December wind they could hear whipping up outside.

At the moment, however, it felt nice and cozy. Carol stood there, gazing out the large, double-pane windows she'd installed in the wall where the garage doors used to be. They provided the light she needed for her intricate work and a fantastic view of the mountain landscape surrounding her home, a landscape now frosted with brilliant white snow.

She turned to find Bobbi grinning at her. Bobbi was a brown-eyed brunette, a good foot shorter than Carol and a few pounds heavier. That didn't mean she was even slightly plump, however, for Carol Applegate was slender as a reed, a tall, willowy woman with blue eyes and shoulder-length hair so blonde it was nearly the color of fresh cream. The combination gave her an almost angelic appearance, while in comparison Bobbi looked like an impish forest sprite.

Especially when she grinned in this particularly wicked way. Carol sighed. "What now?"

"Just wondering if you've discovered anything else on Mr. Richard Palance that's as sensitive as his ego," Bobbi replied. "Was he by any chance the inspiration for that statue's impressive masculine charms?"

"Roberta Cathecart!" Carol glared at her. "I've only known the man a couple of weeks, for heaven's sake!"

"During which he's taken you to almost every lavish restaurant in the Rocky Mountains," Bobbi pointed out. "I figure there has to be something really special about Palance for you to drop Sean O'Phaelan from your social calendar."

"And you think it's something sexual, naturally."

Bobbi's grin broadened. "Naturally. He's extremely handsome. And then there's the way he came on to you from the moment he saw you—a come-on you didn't seem to mind, I might add."

"He was just being nice."

"Nice? If he'd been touching instead of looking, you would've had fingerprints from head to toe."

"So he's attracted to me. So I am not immune to the appreciation of a handsome, worldly man. That doesn't mean I jumped into bed with him at the first opportunity," Carol objected. "Some people do have other things on their mind than sex, Bobbi. I suppose you hadn't noticed he's also extremely rich."

"And that can be quite an aphrodisiac, from what I hear. But Sean O'Phaelan is hardly a pauper, either. In any case, if you want my opinion—"

"I don't."

"No matter what's going on between you and Palance, I think it's a damn shame," Bobbi continued. "You already had the most eligible bachelor around here right in the palm of your hand. Heck, rumor has it Sean was about to pop the question. How could you throw it all away on a fling?"

Carol put on one of the thick leather aprons, carefully avoiding the other woman's eyes. The two of them had been friends long before

Carol's artwork began selling well enough for her to afford to hire Bobbi as a helper. She usually counted herself lucky that their feelings for each other hadn't changed since they started working together.

But there were occasions, such as right now, when she wished they weren't so close. Though she had a great time listening to Bobbi's amorous antics, discussing her own love life was another matter entirely. In fact, it always made her distinctly uncomfortable.

"Maybe it's more than a fling," Carol replied at last.

"Who are you kidding? I would never be unfaithful to my husband, but you may have noticed I take great delight in studying the opposite sex. Richard Palance is not the sort to make a commitment, Carol. What do you hope to gain by dumping a man who loves you in favor of one who'll move on as soon as he gets what he wants out of you?" Bobbi chortled. "Or should I say *into* you?"

Carol didn't answer. Instead, she reached over and turned on the overhead blower. Its whirring din joined the noise of the melting-pot furnace, making normal conversation all but impossible.

"Dammit!" Bobbi yelled. "This has something to do with your ex-husband, doesn't it?"

"I can't hear you!" Carol yelled back.

"It's December, he's about due to drop by for his usual Christmas handout, and you're getting into your usual bizarre Christmas mood!" Bobbi was practically screaming now. "You can't let one bad experience put you off love forever, Carol!"

"Bah! Humbug!"

"Scrooge!"

Flipping her face shield down, Carol pointed to the foundry, indicating it was time to work, not talk. Bobbi scowled at her, then began preparing the mountain lion molds to receive their dose of molten bronze. The work they were about to do was as dangerous as it was hot, and required their full concentration.

Which suited Carol just fine. She needed the respite from Bobbi's sincere and well-meaning but unwanted advice. It didn't help any that she knew, deep down, that her friend was right about one thing at least.

Carol Applegate may have spent a fair number of her thirty-two years with her shoulder to the proverbial wheel, but not one hour of it had been in a cold, dark counting house. She was frugal, but hardly a miser. If her view of mankind as a whole was not particularly rosy, neither was it so bleak that she kept her own company exclusively. There were many people other than Bobbi she called friend, and many more who were pleased to have made her acquaintance.

Nevertheless, Carol was indeed a Scrooge. But it wasn't Christmas she considered a humbug. It was love. And the bizarre mood Bobbi had noticed was a time-honored tradition.

The holidays had always been special for her,

particularly as a young girl. It wasn't just the presents, although finding lovely things beneath the tree was as much a delight to her as to any other child. Her favorites were those things bestowed upon her by dear Uncle Fred, who specialized in much-coveted, parentally frowned upon gifts. One year, she recalled, it had been a pair of pearl-handled cap pistols, which her mother abhorred and with which Carol had terrorized the neighborhood for months.

But the best ever was a shiny, vicious-looking set of razor-sharp woodworking knives. That was the year her mother had to replace the dining-room table—and that Uncle Fred decided he'd better give clothing from then on.

More than the gifts and goodies, however, even better than a vacation from school or the annual family ritual of picking out the perfect tree, young Carol had loved Christmas for the changes it brought. There was always a special feeling to the holiday, a magical, mystical, anything-can-happen sort of feeling. In some ways it seemed a more important rite of passage than a birthday to her. On her birthday she was officially a year older; on Christmas the world itself prepared to turn another page.

Change. Something new, different, and exciting. That was what Christmas really meant to her. After all the pretty presents were opened and all the sugar cookies in festive shapes consumed, the air still held its sparkle, fairly danced with golden dreams of a new year.

Of course, she soon found that change was a knife that cut both ways. Each new year also took Carol another step closer to the occasionally harsh realities of adulthood. Nap times turned into study halls. College proved to be less of a breeze than high school had been. Then came that first real job and an apartment of her own, replacing the easy life of a dorm room and money from home. The ultimate dream of all children had at last materialized; as everyone must, Carol had become a grown-up.

Still, she tried to keep Christmas in her heart, even though it sometimes seemed as if every ill wind that blew her way arrived with a dusting of snow and jingle bells.

Take Frank, for instance. She'd met him on a group skiing trip, and felt certain she had found true love at last. The road leading into the future didn't seem quite so daunting with someone to hold her hand. So, with a festive Yuletide wedding no less, off they went into the matrimonial breach, together to learn the lessons life had to teach.

Unfortunately, one of those lessons was that some people didn't grow up after all. Like her, Frank was a dreamer. Unlike her, he didn't know when to stop dreaming and face facts. The fact Carol had to face was that she had married a child, a boy in the shape of a man, to whom every day was Christmas. While she struggled to make ends meet, he placed his faith in one get-rich-quick mining scheme after another, waiting for Santa Claus to make him a present of success.

Instead, two years to the day after they'd strolled down the aisle, he discovered a surprise of a different sort tucked into his stocking. Divorce papers. A rather bitter statement, perhaps, but it did prove that Carol still held dear at least one of her childhood beliefs—Christmas was a time for change.

Frank took their divorce amiably enough. Then again, he hadn't actually grasped the concept. Carol never knew when she might come home to find him parked on her doorstep. But it was usually at Christmas. And he was usually broke. So, although Carol never went so far as to say she'd like to see him boiled in his own pudding, she did occasionally let loose with a couple of famous expletives. Bah! Humbug!

Nevertheless, this year as always, home, hearth, and now her hard-won studio were decorated for the holidays. Her Scrooginess did not manifest itself in parsimony, in reality had very little to do with money. Carol might never be a Michelangelo, but Uncle Fred had started something with his gift of those woodworking tools long ago.

After college, while eking out an existence as a bookkeeper for a chain of welding shops in Denver, she had spent all her free time learning to sculpt salable items from wood, steel, and stone. Two years with Frank took their toll in both cash and creative energy, but once she had him out of the way—at least most of the time—she finally saved enough to realize her own dream. She moved to the little mountain town of Tithe, Colorado; bought a house and converted the garage to a studio; and now made a fairly decent living as an artist.

Though Carol had done some spectacular pieces and was beginning to build a reputation as a serious sculptor, the mainstays of her business were still those modestly priced, artsy-craftsy sort of things people often bought as gifts, so the Christmas season was her best. She had every reason, therefore, to be filled with Christmas spirit.

Which she was. But just as Bobbi had been right about her being a special type of Scrooge, she was also right about her being in a special kind of mood; Carol was getting ready to make yet another of her unusual holiday changes.

Sean O'Phaelan was a fun, witty, gregarious bear of a man, certainly eligible, and a successful entrepreneur to boot. There was some doubt as to whether a man who had named his busy roadside pub The Naked Waitress was quite right in the head, but Carol liked him. A lot. That was the problem. Ever mindful of the mistake she'd made with Frank, Carol wasn't sure she wanted to like anybody this much again.

Then, too, she'd been doing a lot of thinking about her alternatives since Richard Palance had arrived on the scene.

Where Sean was quite handsome, Richard was an absolute lady killer. Granted, he was rather forbidding, with his dark, searing eyes and mysterious demeanor. And there was something disturbing about the way he'd just seemed to appear in town one day, like a wraith on the cold winter breeze.

Nevertheless, as her ever-watchful friend Bobbi had noticed, Richard made it obvious he was very taken with Carol from the moment he stepped foot in her studio, and hadn't let up since. It was also obvious he was very willing to use his considerable wealth to win her.

While that was a tantalizing notion to a woman who had known the economic downside of life, it was not, however, the main attraction.

Nor was it sex. Carol wasn't sure comparisons were fair or even possible on that score. It was all so relative. She'd thought the world of a lover she'd had in college, until she met Frank. Frank couldn't hold a candle to Sean, big Irish bull that he was. In fact—though she'd never tell Bobbi—it was Sean who had served as model for the well-endowed statue standing on her workbench. Of course, such was her confusion that she was doing her best to resist Sean's advances anyway, so the point was moot.

As for Richard, she'd told Bobbi the truth; she hadn't jumped into bed with him at the first opportunity, or any of the subsequent opportunities he went out of his way to provide. But even if their relationship hadn't progressed to complete intimacy yet, Carol had a feeling he would prove considerably more than competent.

If she was to be honest with herself—something she rarely was these days—Carol would have admitted that the real reason she found Richard so beguiling was the very one Bobbi was taking such pains to point out to her. Carol knew he didn't have the slightest intention of making a commitment. In her jaded opinion, that was much safer than a relationship that might actually lead somewhere, such as love and marriage.

No doubt about it, Carol had a problem with the *L* word. And why not? Love had made a fool of her more than once. Which was why she tried to keep her heart as tightly locked as old Ebenezer had his pocketbook.

Yes, Sean was in love with her, and she had started to feel some leanings in that direction herself. But she and Frank had been in love too. So what if in comparison to Sean's easy, spontaneous way with her, Richard's approach was almost methodical? She'd been married to the king of spontaneity and had no desire to repeat the experience.

So to Carol the choice was clear. A change. Something new and different. And Christmas was the time for change.

2

Nestled in an isolated canyon of the Colorado Rockies, the mountain hamlet of Tithe—like countless others of its ilk—had started its diverse and colorful history as that singular, often nameless entity known as a boomtown. Silver was this one's main claim to fame, though greater fortunes were made by those who sold goods and services to hopeful prospectors than by the prospectors themselves.

Particularly on Saturday nights. After a hard week at their digs, miners would come in for a night on whatever ragtag grouping of tents and buildings passed for a town in their vicinity. These sprees usually included a drink or two, a few rolls of the dice, then a visit to another sort of sporting house for a roll of a different kind altogether.

The one asset that set this particular community apart from the rest was its church, the only one for miles around. Whether out of guilt, religious fervor, or simply to hedge their bets, Sunday morning would usually find those same miners in that church, putting a portion of what was left of their silver and gold in the collection plate.

Tithe had undergone considerable change since its glory days. There were still miners about, but silver had long since been replaced as a priority in favor of oil shale, coal, and other less precious ores, so with the exception of one or two grizzled old prospectors searching for the mother lode, most of them worked for the big mining conglomerates. On average they were married, had children, drank in moderation, and confined their gambling to the purchase of an occasional lottery ticket. And these days, the only sort of sporting ladies around played a wicked game of softball.

Other than the church, which still survived by the grace of its tithing members, about the only thing that remained the same was the town's philosophy. There was still a booming business in providing goods and services. While not exactly on a direct route to anywhere, Tithe was a worthwhile and even necessary detour for those who came to fish or run rapids in summer, ski in winter, and take in the beautiful scenery year round.

It was a peaceful town now, with a pleasant assortment of shops, restaurants, and inns for the weary traveler. But a town, like a person, can never totally shake its past, especially one that had been as bold and bawdy as Tithe's.

Small mountain villages attracted a certain type of resident to begin with. Carol was not the only artist who made her home there, nor was she alone in her bizarre moods and unusual traditions. Though not as wild as the shopkeepers and miners of old, many did share their zest for life as well as a certain tendency toward eccentricity. For instance, one successful inn took great pride in advertising a fact that to some might have been an embarrassment—the establishment's heritage as a brothel.

Then there was The Naked Waitress pub.

Located just off the main road through town, the building itself seemed locked in a time warp. Built of native stone and hand-hewn timber, it predated what scant records remained from the boomtown era and was generally assumed to be one of Tithe's oldest structures. As such, its stout walls had no doubt seen a great deal, but they weren't talking.

Most considered that a blessing. The glory days, after all, hadn't always been so glorious. What mattered was that it was now not only one of the oldest, but one of the finest buildings in town, and a happy one as well. If the walls did decide to speak, they would probably have as many nice things to say about the man responsible for this dramatic change as everyone else in Tithe.

When Sean O'Phaelan bought the place seven years ago, it had been boarded up for twice that long, so was in need of much repair. This he did with the stoicism of his Irish forebears, little by little as time and money allowed, all the while building both a profitable business and his own impeccable reputation. The only minor glitch in an otherwise completely honest operation was its name.

As far as Sean was aware—and he was aware of everything that happened in his pub—there had never been so much as one breast bared in The Naked Waitress, male or female. At least not of flesh and blood. The ancient wood carving above the bar was another matter. Predictably, it was entitled *A Maid in Waiting*. Sean knew some thought him crazy for bending the truth in advertising laws, and so he was. Crazy like a fox.

Everyone who drove through town saw the titillating name on the front of his pub; nearly everyone who saw it stopped to see what was going on inside. And 99 percent of those who stopped saw that the joke was on them, had a good laugh, then stayed for a beer or one of the simple but hearty meals offered on the modest menu. The place had cleared a tidy profit by its third year.

There were, of course, a few who resented being fooled, but a free drink and the laughter of what was usually a large crowd of more good-natured folk almost always put things right. On those very rare occasions when some poor perverted soul with more hormones than brains took a notion to create his own naked waitress from scratch, one look at Sean O'Phaelan changed his mind.

Sean was as strongly built as the building that housed his pride and joy. He stood six three in his stocking feet, weighed two twenty-five completely dry, and had no end of trouble with his wardrobe. Not that he was fat. Far from it. To fit his chest he bought extra-large shirts, then had to have them altered so they'd fit his trim thirty-four-inch waist without bagging like a ship's sails. When he bought jeans that were snug on his slender hips and buttocks, they had a tendency to cut off the circulation in his muscular thighs.

Needless to say, Sean was on very good terms with the local tailor. With the exception of any man who dared bother his waitresses, he was on good terms with almost everybody. He was as kind and gentle in disposition as he was large of physique. Women in particular were fond of Sean, with his sparkling green eyes, wavy auburn hair, and chiseled features.

Though he'd been a bit of a rogue in his youth, he'd settled down some as he neared forty and was looking to settle down even more. Toward that end, Sean had eyes for only one woman these days. Unfortunately, that woman had suddenly started looking in another direction.

"It's a damn shame, I tell you," a gray-haired man sitting at the bar announced. "A crying shame."

Sean cleared away the man's empty glass, carefully wiping up the ring of moisture it had left on the shiny maple bar. Then he poured the man another beer, placed it in front of him, and reduced his pile of change by seventy-five cents.

"There you go, Jack," Sean said. "That'll give you something to cry into."

"Thanks." He sipped it. "Join me?"

"In the beer? Or the tears?"

The older man laughed. "Take your pick."

"I don't feel the need of either one today, thanks."

"Whatever you say, son." He gazed at Sean, his pale-blue eyes bright with curiosity. "I'll be around if you change your mind."

Nodding, Sean moved back down the bar to tend his other customers. Lunch had been busy, as usual, but the rush was over and the pub fairly quiet. Like any other business owner, Sean would have preferred to see his establishment overflowing, but he appreciated times such as this too. It gave him a chance to catch his breath, total the day's receipts, and take a look out the window to see what the rest of Tithe was up to this fine winter day.

He could see practically the entire town through the pub's big plate-glass window. Snow was falling, big, puffy flakes, adding a fresh layer of white to replace what the sun had melted that morning. In its protected valley, Tithe rarely got the huge accumulations common at higher elevations. Instead it spent most of the winter beneath a fairly constant foot-thick blanket. At Christmastime, especially, the place looked like a picture postcard or a print by Currier and Ives.

Every building, including the pub, was decked out for the holidays. There were groups of children all over, making snowmen, sledding, or simply celebrating their temporary freedom from school with a dizzy romp. A snowball fight was raging in the middle of town, Sean noticed, with bunkers for the opposing forces set up on the rock-strewn hills lining either side of Tithe's main street. Elliot Parker, supermarket manager, came out and shook his fist at the combatants, obviously concerned about those occasional misfires landing in his parking lot. Laughing children scattered in every direction, only to regroup and start all over a block down.

"Having quite a time out there."

Sean turned his attention from the window and saw that Jack had moved down the bar to join him. "That they are. Makes you wish you were a kid again."

"Or had some of your own to make you feel like one," Jack said. His smile and prickly gray beard gave him the look of a sly old fox. "I tell you it's—"

"A crying shame," Sean completed. "You're starting to repeat yourself, Jack."

"Us old farts are allowed to do that, son. It's a rule. So is filling a man's glass when he's still thirsty."

Jack Bensen was a small man, wiry and thin, and if he'd driven to The Naked Waitress Sean wouldn't even consider serving him a third beer so soon. But in the first place he didn't own a car, and in the second he was a man of habit.

Jack would take that last beer over to the pool

tables, coax someone—usually Sean—into a game of eight ball while he finished it, and then switch to ice water. The beer was to loosen up his shooting arm, and unless his arthritis was particularly bad, he wouldn't have another drink or pay for another game. Whatever change he had left from the five dollars he'd walked in with would remain on the bar as a tip.

Sean also knew that Jack Bensen could ill afford to leave that money behind. A miner all his life, he still worked a small claim west of town, where he lived in a cabin he'd built with his own two hands. If gold hadn't taken such a sharp rise in price, there was no way he could have survived on the tiny amount of dust he pulled out of the ground. As it was, he could manage the bare necessities and the luxury of his visits to the pub, and that was all.

But he wouldn't accept charity. Nor would Sean offend him by offering it. What he did was take Jack's change, add some of his own as well as that of whomever else cared to chip in, and put it in a big Mason jar. When it was full, that meant it was time for another infamous semitriannual Tithe invitational billiard tournament and covered-dish supper, with the jar and any leftover food going to the winner.

Jack always won. Of course, the tournaments were only open to locals and there wasn't a player in town he couldn't beat, but that didn't mean anybody let him win. They didn't have to. Sean liked the elderly pool shark and would have let him hang around The Naked Waitress whether he ever spent a nickel in the place or not. But the fact was, he was good at the game, so good that tourists and locals alike stayed to challenge him or just to watch him play.

In other words, Jack Bensen brought in a lot of business. With his flamboyant style and endless supply of riveting tales from the good old, bad old days, he was as much a draw for The Naked Waitress as its name, good food, and low prices.

He was also Tithe's most efficient snoop. Sean hadn't taken the bait yet, but he knew full well that Jack wasn't feeling sorry for himself. The crying shame he kept trying to get Sean to comment on was what everyone in town was now calling Applegate, as in Watergate, with one Richard Palance cast in the role of chief dirty trickster.

True to his routine, Jack stood up and took his beer over to his favorite of the two small, coin-operated pool tables located on either side of the pub's rear entrance. He put in his quarter, listened to the balls drop, then racked them expertly at one end of the table's green felt surface. As he selected a cue, he looked around him.

"Anybody for a game of eight ball?"

None of the locals appeared quite ready to take him on just yet, and this close to Christmas there weren't many strangers passing through. The only two people in the pub he didn't recognize were a young man and woman on their way home from a skiing trip; it was quite obvious what they were interested in, and it certainly wasn't pool.

"How about it, Sean?" Jack asked.

"Sure. Won't be a minute." He finished up the glasses he'd been washing and dried his hands. "Everybody okay for now?" The patrons all signaled they were, so he came out from behind the bar to join his friend at the pool table.

"I'll even let you break," Jack said.

"Magnanimous of you."

Sean chalked his cue and bent over the table to take aim. Just as he was about to stroke, Jack cleared his throat and asked, "Seen Carol lately?"

CRACK!

The cue ball hit the rack with so much force that it jumped clear off the table, skipped twice on the bar, and landed in a woman's lap on the far side of the room. Two other balls likewise took flight, bounced, then went rolling across the polished wood floor in opposite directions. Of those remaining on the table, three went into pockets and the rest were pressed to the rails, where they sat spinning like brightly colored tops for a few seconds afterward.

"Godalmighty!" Jack was laughing so hard he could barely speak. "A simple yes or no would have done, boy!"

Sean went to gather up the wayward billiard balls, apologizing profusely as he did so. He replaced them on the table and handed the cue ball to Jack, giving him the evil eye at the same time.

"Your shot, you low-down snake."

Jack was still laughing. "I take it you either haven't seen her, or you have and she gave you the cold shoulder."

"She's been busy."

"Sure she has."

"It is only two days till Christmas, Jack. Carol has a business to run. So do I."

As he talked, the older man played pool, thus combining the two things he loved to do most in the world. "Horse crap. You're not fooling anyone. And by the way you just clobbered these balls, I'd say it's been eating at you some. Nine ball, off the eleven, corner pocket." He deftly made the shot just as he'd called it. "If she's so all-fired busy, how is it she has the time to go out with Palance?"

Unless Jack decided to go easy on him, Sean knew he probably wouldn't get another shot. He knew for sure he was in for a discussion about Carol no matter what. So he went to the bar and got his toolbox, then sat down with a heavy sigh to repair the cue tip he'd just ruined. Maybe the old boy was right in trying to get him to talk. It might settle his case of the jitters.

"Palance is an okay guy."

"Okay?" Jack slammed another ball home. "He's trying to steal your woman, son!"

Sean looked up at him. "All right. So he's shit. But Carol's got a mind of her own. I know what you and everyone else around here would like to see me do—"

"Damn straight!" Jack interrupted. "Everybody in town likes you two. And we were pretty darn sure you loved each other."

"I do love her," Sean said. "But Carol . . . Well, she's a cautious one. That no-account she was married to hardened her heart. I did think I was winning her over, though."

"So did we. Eleven ball in the side, one bank." It fell with a *thunk.* "Hell, we thought we were fixing to have us a wedding. Then Mr. Fancypants Palance showed up. *Him* we don't love. I for one would like to shove a stick of dynamite up his butt and light the fuse."

Sean shook his head and laughed. "Sure, but you're a hard man, Jack. Haven't you heard? This is a kind and gentle nation we're living in now."

"Bullsquat! Tell that to the miners on the western slope. You'll find a good many in the unemployment line. And don't go changing the subject on me." He paused to study a tricky shot, called it, then made it. "We're talking about what you're going to do with Palance."

"I'm not going to do anything with him. It has to be Carol's decision," Sean told him. "That's what I was trying to say. I know the whole town would love to see me kick his ass clear to Denver, but it just isn't going to happen."

Jack sighed. "I never thought I'd see the day. Not that I blame you, mind. He's a scary one. Too quiet by far for my taste. And those eyes, dark and hard like a couple of obsidian chips." He shivered. "Still . . ."

"Is that what everybody thinks?" Sean asked. "That I'm afraid of him?"

"Aren't you?"

"Hell no!"

Sean stood up, an unconscious reaction to being called a coward that served its purpose nicely. Men of his size seldom actually had to fight. Other than a complete idiot or steroid abuser—one and the same—few would care to carry an argument with him that far.

"Then what's the problem?" Jack wanted to know. "In my day, if you caught a man jumping your claim you stomped him flat and rode him out of town on a rail."

"Men don't settle their differences that way anymore, Jack. At least I don't, although I will admit to being sorely tempted in this case. But in the first place I don't fancy spending Christmas in jail, and in the second it wouldn't accomplish a damn thing. Except to drive Carol farther away from me," Sean added. "I can't bully my way back into her life. Like I said, she has a mind of her own, and she'll make it up on her own. I know the type of man Palance is; hell, I used to *be* his type. Bed 'em and begone. Sooner or later Carol will realize that's not what she really wants."

"Sooner or later!" Jack exclaimed. "Christ! You can't just stand by and let the woman you love get taken advantage of! Carol Applegate may be every bit as stubborn as my moth-eaten mule, but there has to be something you can do. If you're not going to punch the guy's lights out, at least stand fast. How can you expect her to choose the right horse if she's been too long out of the saddle?" He tapped a corner pocket with the tip of his cue, lined up his shot, and sunk the eight ball. "Ha! You've staked your claim, now work the vein!"

Sean smiled. "I intend to."

"I knew it!" Jack put his cue stick on the table and came to stand beside Sean, cackling gleefully. "I knew you weren't going to slink away with your tail between your legs. Tell old Jack all about it."

"There's nothing to tell. Tomorrow night is Christmas Eve, that's all. Carol doesn't know it yet, but I'm going to spend it with her, making sure she has all the information she needs for this decision."

Jack was clearly disappointed. "Well, shit. That's a start, I suppose, but not exactly what I had in mind. You know Palance is bound to show up too."

"I'm certain he'll make an appearance."

"So there is going to be a fight!"

"Not unless he starts one," Sean said.

"Of all the fool . . ." Jack trailed off in an exasperated sigh. "Use your head, Sean. You can't put two young bucks in with a skittish doe and not have some kind of confrontation."

Again, Sean just smiled. "I didn't say there wouldn't be a confrontation. But I doubt it'll turn violent. Carol's the one with the problem, not us, and Palance and I are both too mature to think butting heads will solve it. She's the only one who can do that."

"In case you hadn't noticed, she's been leaning pretty heavily in the direction of Richard Palance for the last two weeks," Jack informed him. "Providing you can get some time alone with her, don't you think you're putting an awful lot of faith in your ability to win her back in just one night?"

"Oh, I don't know," Sean replied, shrugging his broad shoulders. "It's Christmas. I suppose you could say I'm counting on her to have a change of heart."

"Son, you better ask Santy Claus to bring you a new brain. The one you got is plumb wore out."

3

"The Patterson transaction finally made it past the lawyers, with the check to be wired directly to your Swiss account. Watanabi Steel is predicted to rise four points after the first of the year; Tokyo is keeping an eye on it for you, and I'll be keeping an eye on them. Let's see. Arrangements for your presentation to the American Ski Team are all set, except for delivery of the statue. You're certain you wish to handle that yourself, sir?"

"I am. The piece will be delicate. No offense, Stevens, but if you want something done right . . ."

"I understand completely, sir. No offense taken."

Richard Palance leaned back in his chair, gazing at the ceiling. Except for the heavy redwood beams overhead, this room of the mountainside condo he'd rented for his stay in Tithe was startlingly familiar. It amazed him how Stevens could carve out a niche for them wherever they went, set up a working environment so similar to all the other temporary offices they'd occupied over the past year. In what generic warehouse did he find the same type of chrome and black leather chairs, mahogany desks, and computer terminals that seemed magically to find their way to each new location?

But then, office furniture was undoubtedly just another of the many things his personal secretary had taken upon himself to standardize in his effort to reduce mental clutter. Stevens was constantly on the lookout for distractions. It was part of the man's job, Richard supposed, but in his opinion he was getting a tad too overzealous.

There was only one distraction Richard was interested in at the moment, and as soon as this end-of-the-day update was finished, he planned to give it his full attention no matter how miffed his secretary got with him.

"Anything else?" he asked.

Stevens pushed his glasses to the end of his nose and peered at him over the top of the rims, smiling. "Just one more thing. I canceled your morning appointment with Faraday, Best, and Whittaker on the twenty-seventh and rescheduled for the following afternoon."

"Oh, yes." Richard smiled too. "Did they scream?"

"Loudly, sir. They reminded me that they must have your signature before the first. I assured them you were well aware of that fact."

"Good." He nodded, still studying the redwood beams. "Let the bastards sweat. By the way, you did clear my calendar for the twenty-sixth?"

"I did." Closing the notebook he held in his lap, Stevens cleared his throat, then stood up. "Taking an extended holiday this year, sir?" He seemed to disapprove. "Not on my account, I trust."

"No, Stevens. Not on your account. I simply plan to enjoy Christmas to the fullest and may need the day after to recuperate." Richard's dark eyes sparkled at some private thought. "My dinner reservations are confirmed for this evening at the . . . What is that silly name again?"

"The Aerie. As in a high nest. Because it's connected with the Highland Hawk ski area, I would presume."

"Ah, yes. Silly name, fantastic chef. Truly memorable trout. My reservations?"

"You and the lady are expected at seven." Again a vaguely disapproving look crossed his narrow face. "As your personal secretary, Mr. Palance, I feel obliged to point out that your concentration seems to have slipped a notch or two as of late. With our plans at such a critical point, I am duty bound to protest. This sculptor—"

"Is none of your business," Richard inter rupted sharply.

He leaned forward to fix the other man with his own look of disapproval. It was one he'd cultivated to such a degree that his secretary was actually driven a step back, as if hit by physical force. Among other things, Richard Palance was a master of intimidation; one did not make it to his position of wealth and power without learning how to act the part of a formidable adversary.

But then he seemed to catch himself. He let out a deep breath and started to laugh. "Stevens! I am sorry. I know you only have my best interests at heart. To be fair, though, you've been driving me so hard I was bound to snap at you eventually."

"I've been worried about you, sir. The end of the year is always such a trial, with so many details, and with the added importance of our business here . . . I only want to ensure nothing slips past us because of some little . . ." He paused, carefully choosing his words. "As you said, I was simply looking after your best interests as I have done these many years. That's all."

"And I appreciate it. But there's a limit to even my endurance. And yours," Richard added. "We've both been working too hard. Christmas is upon us, Stevens! We must take some time to enjoy the finer things in life."

Stevens was staring at him. "She has had an alarming influence on you, you know. And I'm not sure I like it. Nor do I like the idea of being stuck in this snow-covered bastion of disrespectful hicks for a moment longer than is necessary."

"This is a small town, Stevens. You can't expect them to embrace strangers, especially ones such as ourselves. The nature of our business requires us to be discreet; it's only natural for them to be suspicious."

He frowned. "With all due respect, sir, you haven't exactly helped our position in that regard. By spending time with Carol Applegate, I'm given to believe you're stepping on someone's toes; indeed, that appears to be the source of much of the animosity around town."

"That someone would be Sean O'Phaelan," Richard said. "I've met the man. Admirable business acumen. But I hardly bashed Carol over the head and dragged her away from him. In fact, from the way she speaks of Mr. O'Phaelan I gather she was feeling smothered by their relationship and was about to send him packing anyway."

"How convenient for you. Still—"

"My God, man!" Richard cried, getting to his feet. "Isn't there one ounce of romance in your soul? We get so little time to enjoy ourselves, you and I. Perhaps if you stop being such a prig you could find someone to spend the holiday with yourself. Maybe you could even learn a thing or two from the people of Tithe." He came around the desk and clapped the other man on the back. "Lighten up!"

Stevens coughed. "I'll try, sir, but I'm afraid it simply isn't in my nature. Will there be anything else?"

"The cleaners delivered my blue suit?"

"It's in your closet. And the car has a full tank." He turned on his heel and started out of the makeshift office, then stopped and added, "You may regret not renting a four-wheel drive. Tonight should be clear, but the weather report is calling for quite a bit of snow tomorrow evening, perhaps a foot or more."

"That much!" Richard shook his head. "The power of the elements in these mountains is certainly a force to be reckoned with. But Tithe seems to escape the brunt of it, and I'm sure the local road crews will continue to do the fine job they've been doing." He rubbed his hands together in anticipation. "My shopping expedition to Denver tomorrow shouldn't take long. I'm sure I'll be back before dark. And I have much cozier things in mind for Christmas Eve than a moonlight drive. So let it snow!"

"If you say so," Stevens said uncertainly. "I wish you would allow me to make this trip for you."

"You're like a mother hen! Stop worrying and enjoy your three days off. Read some fiction, get out and breathe the fresh mountain air, maybe walk into town tomorrow and visit that pub I told you about. It has a nice bitter ale and a couple of pocket billiard tables, you know."

He sniffed disdainfully. "I prefer snooker."

"I'm losing patience with you, Stevens," Richard told him. "Go have fun! That's an order."

"Yes, sir." He opened the office door. "I'll be right across the courtyard if you need me for anything."

"Out!"

Richard heard his secretary's crisp footsteps on the marble tile of the foyer, then the sound of the front door opening and closing. Smiling, he left the office himself and went upstairs to shower and dress for his dinner with Carol. He hadn't planned on lecturing Stevens, so he would have to hurry. It was only five-thirty, and the restaurant wasn't far, but perhaps if he got to her house early, he would catch her in some charming state of dishabille.

"Be patient, Richard," he cautioned himself.

Although there had been an instant attraction between them, Carol was the sort who needed delicate handling, and he the sort who knew the value of steady, deliberate pressure above rash action. The art of seduction, after all, was not unlike that of conducting a successful business campaign.

He had wined her and dined her, showed her that he was a man of refinement and taste—all the while letting her know he was still very much a man. The refreshing thing about Carol Applegate was that she seemed perfectly aware of the type of liaison Richard had in mind. Indeed, as long as the proper courtesies were observed, it was apparently what she was after as well. No games, other than the sweet teasing of getting to know each other; no search for meaning higher than that of enjoying the pleasure of one another's company.

Tonight, after a leisurely dinner, he would take her back to the condo for a nightcap. Some soft music, perhaps even a dip in the hot, soothing waters of the whirlpool spa if she was of a mind. It was quite possible she would then take the situation into her own hands and lead him to bed, but Richard wasn't depending on that delightful turn of events. He wouldn't object, of course, but neither would he give her any reason to think he expected it. The whole point of this evening wasn't sex, but trust.

But tomorrow evening . . . Well, that would be different. Richard was counting on the warmth and magic of Christmas Eve to cast the final spell. Champagne, firelight, an exchange of gifts—and then, at long last, the exchange of passion they had both been working toward.

4

"What a day!"

"And how," Carol agreed. "Thanks for staying late. I know you're anxious to get home to David."

"You bet I am." Bobbi took off her heavy apron with a sigh of relief. "But he won't even touch me until I've had a bath. I'll bet we smell like a couple of pigs."

"Probably." Her eyes suddenly went wide. "Oh, my God! What time is it?" Carol had known it was past her helper's quitting time because it was dark outside. Since wearing metal against the skin when working around a foundry wasn't advisable, however, she'd removed her watch. She dashed to the workbench and grabbed it. "Shit! It's nearly six and I have a date with Richard tonight!"

Bobbi yawned. "So what else is new?"

As usual at the end of a busy day, the studio was a mess. Carol had always disliked untidiness, but during her brief marriage she'd learned to loathe it, the result of Frank's penchant for leaving beer cans, ore samples, and his filthy prospecting equipment wherever he felt like it.

"It's appropriate we smell like pigs," Carol said, "because this place certainly resembles a sty." She looked at her watch again. "Well, it can't be helped. I'll clean it up tomorrow."

"I can come in if you want."

"Nonsense. I'll be working on Richard's sculpture anyway. I don't want to see you back here until after Christmas," Carol told her with mock severity. "Now shoo! I've got to take a shower and figure out what I'm going to wear tonight. He's taking me to the Aerie."

Bobbi arched her eyebrows. "Again? David and I are lucky to go there once a year."

"I'd never been there until Richard took me the first time." She shrugged. "The food is fantastic, but I'm not sure I like the atmosphere. All those waiters hovering around. It's all a bit intimidating."

"So's Richard."

"That's just his public persona," Carol objected. "A man in his profession has to look mean or people think he can be taken advantage of. It's hard for him to drop the act."

"Just what is his profession, anyway?" Bobbi asked.

"Uh . . . high-risk investments, I think. Venture capital, that sort of thing. Richard doesn't like to talk business. Anyway, he's much nicer in private."

"Do tell."

Carol glared at her. "I don't have time to stand here and feed your fantasies. Scat!"

"Yes'm. And thanks again for the Christmas bonus," Bobbi added, patting the back pocket of her jeans. "It'll come in handy. David and I went overboard, as usual."

"You earned it. Give the kids a hug for me."

"Will do. Merry Christmas!"

"Merry Christmas!"

Carol practically shoved her out the studio door, then locked it, turned out the lights, and went into the house. It was an old place, but at least it was neat. As a precaution, she locked the door leading into the attached studio as well, lest Richard get nosy when he arrived and decide to look in on his sculpture. He wasn't fond of clutter, either.

Peeling off clothes as she went, she dashed upstairs to the bathroom. The shower felt great on her tired body; it was a chore to drag herself from beneath the stinging spray. Although her pale blond hair was so fine it dried quickly even without the use of a styling blower, she used it tonight to save time, time she would need to pick through her closet.

Carol was hardly a clotheshorse, and Tithe certainly wasn't Aspen. It was the least formal town she'd ever lived in, and the places and occasions that did call for nicer things were few and far between. Going out with Richard had strained her wardrobe to the limit, which in turn was straining her patience.

"Dammit! Look at this crap!" Skirts and

blouses went flying through the air, landing in unkempt piles all over her bedroom floor. "I simply have to take some time off and go shopping! Too old. Too green. Too small. Too big."

She held a white top and ecru skirt up in front of her and looked in the mirror. Why did everything she own make her look like a bookkeeper? *Because that's precisely what you were for seven years,* she reminded herself. So what was she now? An artist. Carol suddenly had this picture of herself walking into the fancy restaurant wearing a white smock and beret and got a severe case of the giggles.

Richard, however, would not be amused if he arrived and found her still in a towel. Then again, she thought with a sly smile, perhaps he would. Maybe she should just meet him at the door in a negligee and let the pompous waiters at the Aerie intimidate someone else this evening.

"Whoa! Hold on a second!"

She took a seat on her bed. It was a huge old four-poster with curtains that could be drawn all the way around to shut out the light. She used the curtains only when she was feeling particularly in need of complete isolation, but she'd fallen in love with the antique the moment she'd seen its hand-carved posts.

Right now, though, Carol felt like climbing in and drawing those curtains tight. From time to time over the past two weeks, what she could only describe as a panic attack would grip her, causing such a state of confusion in her mind she could scarcely think straight.

No, that wasn't true. She could think, but only about one thing, and it kept jabbing her over and over.

You're making a big mistake.

But what was the mistake? Going out with Richard? She was a single adult, capable of making her own decisions; it was within her rights to date whomever she pleased.

You're spoken for.

No! There weren't any ties on her, at least none she had agreed to. Sean was the one who had started getting so serious. Okay, so she'd seen it coming and hadn't done a thing to stop it. That was the mistake. Her timing was off, that's all; she should have broken up with him long before this. And now her guilty conscience was bawling her out for handling the job so insensitively.

Handling it? You call suddenly avoiding him and taking up with another man handling it? Sounds more like running away, don't you think?

Absolutely not! What did she have to run away from? Sean was the one who had the problem, not her. He should have kept a closer eye on his heart. It wasn't her fault he'd fallen in love. She certainly hadn't fallen in love with him. Going out with Richard proved that.

You're lying to yourself.

"Stop it!" Carol cried, clamping her hands

over her ears in an attempt to block out the sound of her own mind.

It didn't work. The truth was plainly printed on her memory. Clear, indelible truth. She hadn't just seen what was happening to Sean, she'd felt it happening to herself. And she hadn't simply let it happen. She'd encouraged it.

Her only defense was that their relationship had developed in such slow, subtle steps. They'd met not long after she'd moved to Tithe three years ago—only someone with no curiosity at all could resist stopping at a place called The Naked Waitress—and though there had been some mutual interest, nothing had come of it right away. Neither of them had much free time. His pub had been open for four years, a critical point for any business, and she was just taking her first faltering steps as a professional artist.

As a matter of fact, they had seen each other probably no more than six or seven times that year. He'd dropped by her studio once to see what was going on. That was before Carol had lined up shops to handle her work and was selling right out of her own home; Sean picked one of her limited-edition metal castings as a gift for his mother. She in turn had gone to his pub for a drink or a hamburger now and then, when she could afford to go out.

By her second year in Tithe, they were both doing better financially, but still their time was carefully budgeted. Her nights out were more frequent; Sean would occasionally stop by just to say hello; and every now and then they would go skiing or some such with mutual friends. Yet for some reason they never quite managed to find time for a real date.

It wasn't just their businesses, Carol knew. She was leery of men, didn't make a secret of her reluctance to enter another relationship. In a town the size of Tithe, gossip was rife, so Sean knew about her failed marriage to Frank and seemed to understand. He also couldn't help but notice Frank's occasional visits and undoubtedly wondered what was going on.

In a strange way, it was Frank who broke the stalemate between them and brought bud to their romance.

Last Christmas, Frank's presence had been even less wanted than usual. Carol was finally seeing the light at the end of the tunnel. What she called her kitsch was selling well and she'd gotten some pricey orders for more important work. Then Frank's battered old truck came down her driveway. He stepped out with a big grin and wasn't there for more than two minutes before he tried to put the moves on her and get a loan, in that order.

Carol went nuts. She chased him back into his truck with an ax and put a few sizable dents in its tailgate for good measure as he drove away. Deciding she needed a drink and someone to talk to, Carol went to The Naked Waitress.

Sean knew instantly that something was wrong. He took her to his cozy rooms above the pub, held her in his big, strong arms while she cried, then listened to her until the wee hours. That was the night she finally realized how close she and Sean had actually become. Not one real date, no tacit acknowledgment of any feelings other than friendship, and certainly nothing more intimate than a good-night kiss or two, but somehow, there it was. A spark.

Over the past year that spark had become a flame. They *made* time to see each other, dated each other exclusively and slowly, tentatively became lovers. That part of their relationship was fantastic, the most pleasurable sex Carol had ever known. And as the months passed, she could see the seriousness growing in his eyes.

Sean was in love, perhaps had been in love with her for quite some time. Carol wasn't sure she knew how that was supposed to feel anymore, so long had she cut herself off from it, but there was certainly some strong emotion growing in her too. November came, and suddenly she realized he would soon be asking her a question she didn't want to hear. Or at least thought she didn't.

December. Her traditional time of change, for others a time of love, family, and commitment. She was suddenly quite sure Sean was about to propose, probably his way of trying to wipe away the hurt she had endured during other Christmas seasons, such as when she'd divorced Frank.

But the question had yet to be asked. She'd seen to that, by pretending to be so busy she didn't have time for anything else. Actually, now that she had Bobbi to help her this was the easiest Christmas she'd had. Sean probably suspected as much but was so in tune with her moods that he'd given her the space she needed anyway.

That was *his* mistake. If he hadn't backed off, Carol didn't know what would have happened. As it was, she took some time to think things over and came to a conclusion. Love; marriage; the children Sean clearly wanted; these things scared her half to death. When she was with him it all seemed so right; alone with her thoughts and memories, nothing could have seemed more wrong.

Just when she was searching for some answers to ease her confusion, Richard Palance walked into her life. Here was a man whose motives were easy to decipher. In comparison to unraveling the mysteries of her own emotions, the simple alternative Richard was offering her was too tempting to ignore. So she went out with him.

Take that, love! Get thee behind me, commitment!

There was some guilt, a nagging feeling she was being terribly unfair to Sean, but by and large what she felt was freedom, blessed freedom from her own doubts and twisting, turning thoughts.

Until the panic attacks started, that is. Did

she really want to meet Richard at the door in a nightie? One date should have been enough to prove her point; she was not now nor would she ever be ready to get married again. So why had she continued to accept his dinner invitations? What did she hope to accomplish with this teasing, increasingly intimate flirtation?

Maybe Bobbi was right about its being sexual. Richard could indeed be very intimidating, and yet in a way that only made him all the more dangerously attractive. She had admittedly been looking for an escape, but there was now a definite sizzle between them. Was this liaison simply her peaking feminine hormones taking over?

Possibly. She *was* horny. Deny it as she might, the Christmas season did much the same to her as it did to Bobbi. Then again, it wasn't a model of Richard's masculinity she had attached to her gladiator statue, now was it? Just what was she going to do when he made another of his skillful, carefully designed plays for her?

"What you'd better do right now, stupid," she told herself crossly, "is get off your butt and put something on."

Carol went to her closet and grabbed one of the few outfits she hadn't tossed aside, a rose-red dress with spaghetti straps, zip back, and double-ruffle flounced hem. Over it went a matching, double-breasted long jacket that reached to the top of the first ruffle. It was more of a summer look than winter, and definitely made her seem more angelic than her earlier thoughts foretold, but the color was Christmasy enough that she felt she could get away with it. Besides, it was the only dress she owned that Richard hadn't already seen her in.

Not that it mattered. He was so good at undressing her with his eyes that he could undoubtedly tell her what size and brand of bra she wore, so what was the point? Sean had good eyes too, but at least he took some time to enjoy what she had on before he imagined it off. With Richard she often had the feeling he was seeing her naked regardless.

Which brought up another puzzle. She wasn't supposed to like that feeling, but in a way she did. Sean loved sex and so did she, but even when their lovemaking was wild and passionate there was an undercurrent of tenderness. What would it be like to make love with a man who had nothing other than pure, unbridled lust on his mind?

The doorbell rang. "Enough comparisons," Carol muttered. She poked her head out of her bedroom door and yelled, "Just a minute!" down the stairs, then went back into the bathroom for a last look in the mirror.

A Christmas angel looked back at her, complete with oval face, creamy complexion, pale-blond hair, and sparkling blue eyes. Richard would love it. She still didn't know why she cared or whether she even did. Strange way to feel when she was about to go to an expensive restaurant with a man who had enough sexual magnetism to pluck the fillings right out of her teeth.

One way or another, it would be an interesting night.

5

The Aerie was full to capacity, a fact that amazed Carol considering the prices. But she supposed anybody who could afford to spend Christmas at the Highland Hawk ski resort had a different concept of what was expensive. She couldn't imagine what it would be like to pay a hundred and fifty dollars a night for a room, thirty a day for lift tickets, and then drop another hundred or so on dinner, all without batting an eye.

Good, probably. Somehow, though, Carol knew that if she ever made enough to allow her such luxuries, she still wouldn't be as relaxed about it as these people were.

Richard certainly didn't have any trouble. He saw to it that they were conducted to their table immediately, where a bottle of Dom Perignon already awaited them on ice. The wine steward opened it and poured a bubbling measure into their crystal glasses with a flourish, waited a moment for Richard to taste and nod his approval, then disappeared as quietly as he had come. Menus were brought with the same silent efficiency.

While they studied them, caviar appeared in a small cut-crystal bowl with fresh lemon wedges, ground hard-boiled egg, and delicate squares of toast. Carol's head was spinning at the amount he'd already spent before they'd even had dinner, all without lifting a hand or saying a word. Richard simply studied the menu, totally at ease.

No doubt about it, she was impressed. A lot of things impressed her about Richard Palance. His impeccable attire, for one. The blue suit fit him perfectly, accentuating his tall, slender physique, its soft wool fabric conforming to his every move. Just the right amount of white linen showed at the cuffs, always, so the shirt was obviously tailor-made for him as well. Some men looked fussy in white shirts, but not Richard. It was the perfect color for his olive skin tone and flattered his angular face. His tie, muted red silk, completed the look.

Elegant. From his graceful, manicured fingertips to his jet-black, neatly trimmed hair, Richard Palance was an elegant man. Several women shot him admiring, desirous glances—of which he seemed totally unaware—and Carol realized they were the center of attention even in this ritzy crowd. That, too, was impressive.

Then there was the way he ordered for them, in flawless French no less, a language she had studied in college and could never quite get a handle on. Silly, perhaps, with everything else he had going for him, but it was hearing those perverse verb conjugations and difficult sentence structures roll off his tongue that impressed her the most.

Business; languages; his appearance and behavior; in everything he did, Richard worked hard at being the best. Carol had no doubt that would extend to the bedroom. It was an intriguing thought. Daunting as well, even a bit scary in a way, but she couldn't deny her curiosity.

Why, therefore, did she keep thinking about the last time she and Sean had gone out, the quaint little restaurant with its cozy, informal atmosphere and how nice he had looked in his Harris tweed jacket? There hadn't been a tight knot of tension in her stomach that night. Anticipation of what would happen afterward—and had, a truly glorious evening of sensuous give and take—but not this . . . this what?

Fear?

It wasn't everyone's imagination. For all his elegance, there was something mysterious about Mr. Richard Palance. While he wasn't nearly as strong as Sean physically, he had a potent intellect and the force of his will was clearly visible in his hard, flintlike eyes. It had occurred to Carol more than once that she might be flirting with danger, in the form of a man she couldn't control.

But so what? Maybe that was at the root of her discontent; she and Sean were so comfortable together, complemented each other so well. Comfort was good, but shouldn't there be some thrill, some dangerous mystery, not knowing what might happen or when?

"You look pensive, darling," Richard said, his voice a low, soothing balm on her hyperactive imagination. "Isn't the trout to your liking?"

She smiled at him. "Oh, yes! It's perfect. My mind was wandering, that's all." This was Bobbi's fault. She should know better than to discuss her private life with Tithe's biggest worrywart. "I had a rather busy day today."

"I did notice a certain . . . tension." He made a small gesture with his hand and a waiter appeared to refill their champagne glasses. "There. Nothing like fine wine to relax the mind. As for the rest of you," Richard said softly, "a very pleasant idea for a remedy just occurred to me. After dinner, why don't we adjourn to my condominium? The whirlpool there does wonders for tired, overworked muscles."

"No, I don't think so, Richard," Carol replied, touching his forearm to ease any disappointment. "Tomorrow—"

"Is another day. And quite a few hours off. You do look frazzled. Beautiful," he added with a smile that showed his white teeth, "but yours is an amazingly physical profession, after all. You have a perfect right to be tired, and I every right to be concerned about you. The success of my sculpture is in your talented hands. To be sharp upon the morrow, you should relax tonight."

"Well . . ."

Richard took her hand, gently caressing the back of it with a circular movement of his thumb. "A splash of cognac, perhaps, amid the hot, swirling water. Soft music to calm the soul. And then, when you're ready to drift off, I'll return you to your home for a sleep filled not with the workaday world, but pleasant dreams. Doesn't that sound nice?"

So much for disappointment. It was quite apparent to her that Richard didn't have any intention of letting her reject his invitation. What's more, he was a persuasive devil. While he was describing his remedy for stress, she felt her eyelids growing heavy and a sigh escaped her lips.

"Oh, my!" Carol exclaimed softly. "I'd have to be crazy to say no, wouldn't I?"

He chuckled. "Not at all. But it would give me the impression you were even more in need of such therapy than I first presumed, in which case I would be guilty of forsaking a fellow human being should I fail to carry you off and cure you. Surely you wouldn't want that on your conscience?"

The English language flowed as gracefully from his mouth as French. Carol could practically feel his rich, resonant voice dancing upon her skin. Little wonder he was so wealthy; a man like this could have talked Ebenezer Scrooge himself out of his last farthing.

"Goodness, no," Carol replied. But carry her off? A gilded threat was still a threat, wasn't it? Then she decided she was seeing menace where there was only teasing. "Seriously, Richard, it sounds heavenly. But I do have an awful lot of running around to do tomorrow."

"Still you persist?" There was an undercurrent of irritation in his tone now. His dark eyes narrowed slightly, and for a moment Carol thought he was mad at her. But then he said, "Say it isn't so. I've recently been told my concentration is faltering, and now I'm losing my powers of persuasion. I'll be ruined."

"Don't be silly, Richard. You're the most persuasive person I've ever known. And as far as I can tell your concentration hasn't slipped an inch."

That was a gross understatement. When he'd picked her up earlier this evening, his concentration had been focused so fiercely upon her that she wished the bustier she wore beneath her dress were made of lead rather than lace.

"Then what could it be?" Richard asked. "You know I'm a gentleman, or at least I should hope you do by now. I trust you're not falling prey to the gossip around Tithe?"

Carol tried to look innocent. "Gossip?"

"That I carry women and little children off to devour them in my guarded mountaintop lair. If so, then I must insist you come home with me, if only to prove I'm not a heinous beast."

"That's not what they're saying!" Laughing, she removed her hand from beneath his and took a sip of champagne. "The only things I've heard have to do with your business here. And of course that you've stolen me away from Sean

O'Phaelan." He continued to smile, but there was a certain gleam in his eyes that made Carol uneasy. "What's wrong?"

"Why, nothing at all! It's just that I'm afraid I'll have to disappoint you, and that distresses me."

"Disappoint me? In what way?"

"In that I can't lay any rumors to rest concerning my business," Richard replied apologetically. "You know I deal in investments?" She nodded. "Well, investments are delicate things. In order to make money on them, you must keep your interest in whatever it is you wish to invest in to yourself. It does get tricky on occasion. As a matter of fact, it's possible I could even be doing something illegal if I were to divulge any information."

Her eyebrows arched. "You mean like insider trading or something?" she asked in a whisper.

"Or something." He touched his finger to his lips. "You're not disappointed?"

"No! Actually, the mystery is kind of . . . stimulating."

There was no mistaking what made his eyes gleam now. "Which brings us to the second rumor. From what you've told me, I think I did less stealing from Mr. O'Phaelan than I did rescuing." He leaned closer to her and added softly, "And no matter what you call it, I'd do it again, no matter how many tongues it set wagging."

Leave it to Richard to come up with just the right description of what had happened. She'd been rescued from Sean and the commitment he wanted from her.

And just who will rescue you from Richard?

In a vindictive reaction to that unwanted thought tiptoeing across her brain, Carol said, "I accept your invitation. As long as you have me home early. But what about a suit?"

"Suit?" He looked puzzled. "Oh. A bathing suit, you mean. The condo came fully stocked. I'm sure we can come up with something," he assured her blithely. Again, a slight motion of his hand brought a waiter to their table instantly. *"L'addition, s'il vous plait."*

"Oui, Monsieur Palance."

Richard paid the check, tipped the fawning group of waiters lavishly, then took Carol's hand in his own and led her from the dining room.

"Would you excuse me for a moment?" Carol asked.

"Certainly. I'll just have the car brought around."

She crossed the restaurant's spectacular lobby and went down a long ornately decorated hallway to the ladies' lounge. When she emerged awhile later, she noticed a man standing at the end of the hall studying an old grandfather clock. The antique caught her eye as well, so she went to have a look at it. It hadn't been there on her previous visit to the Aerie.

The man smiled at her. "Beautiful, isn't it?"

"Very."

"Listen to it!" he exclaimed in a deep, oddly

soothing voice. "So methodical as it ticks away the seconds of our lives." Then he chuckled. "Wouldn't it be nice if we could turn back the hands of time as easily as we can reset this clock?"

"I'll say," Carol agreed.

After a moment the man turned and walked back down the hallway. Though she should be getting back to the lobby herself, Carol couldn't resist lingering to study the clock as it ticked away a few of those precious seconds he had mentioned. She worked in many media now, from cast bronze to stone and on to direct metal such as the wire sculpture she was doing for Richard, but wood was still her first love.

Made entirely of walnut with brass and ebony trim, the intricately carved cabinet of the grandfather clock called out to her artistic senses, begging to be touched. She stood there, running her fingers along the smooth wood, listening to the steady, unfaltering rhythm of its mechanism.

Tick. Tock. Tick. Tock. Over and over, never ceasing, the constant movement of the gleaming pendulum swinging back and forth in time to the steady beat. It was mesmerizing.

To turn back the hands of time. What would she choose? Childhood, perhaps, so carefree and blissfully dependent on others for the necessities of life. Or maybe the teen years, turbulent but exciting, full of hopes and dreams and that sweet feeling of immortality. Most of the rest she wouldn't care to relive, unless she could change things.

That was the ticket. Turn the hands forward, not back. Go take a look at how the whole crazy thing came out, then return and make sure she did it right.

But then she would be forever second-guessing, wouldn't she? Make a decision, jump ahead to see if it had been the correct one, jump backward and do it over. And over again. It would be hard for a person to enjoy life while bouncing back and forth on the swinging pendulum of time, constantly trying to make improvements.

"Carol?"

She looked up to find that Richard had come searching for her. "Oh! I'm sorry. I was just admiring this clock. Isn't it lovely?"

Richard glanced at it. "Very nice," he said with an indulgent smile. "But it pales next to you. Come, my beautiful, aching artisan. The baths await!"

6

The condominium complex was guarded, but the nice older man at the gate was hardly the type to allow Richard or anyone else to pass by with a kidnap victim tied up in the backseat of their car. Besides, Richard's Porsche didn't really have a backseat. Nor was Carol with him against her will. With a fine meal and a few glasses of champagne inside her, not to mention the thought of a hot whirlpool bath on this cold winter night, she was ready to follow him anywhere.

Well, not *quite* anywhere. As he showed her around the plush abode, with its vaulted ceilings, modern furnishings, and thick wall-to-wall carpet, Carol realized he was saving the bedroom for last. On the stairway to the second level, she suddenly started feeling shaky and almost fell.

"Whoops!"

Richard grabbed her arm to steady her. "All right?"

"Must have caught my heel. I guess I'm too used to wearing sneakers," she said.

"Here, hold on to the banister while I take

these off for you," he instructed, then lowered himself to one knee and started to remove her high heels. "Lift."

"No!"

He glanced up at her. "Come along! Can't have you breaking your neck."

"All right. But I'll do it," Carol told him. She felt like a fool, but for some reason the idea of him taking off her shoes seemed so . . . so familiar. "It's just that my feet are extremely sensitive."

"Oh?" One black eyebrow shot up. "How intriguing."

Carol slipped off her shoes and picked them up in one hand. "There. The whirlpool?"

"Is just off the master bedroom suite," Richard replied. He rose from his knee and continued up the stairs ahead of her, though he turned often to check on her over his shoulder. The expression on his face was more bemused than concerned.

A spa just off the master bedroom. How sybaritic.

You asked for it.

"Uh . . . are you sure you have a suit for me?"

"Certainly." He paused at the top of the stairs until she joined him, then guided her down the hallway, one of his hands resting lightly on her shoulder. "You didn't think I'd let you plunge in naked, did you?"

She managed a small, nervous laugh. "Of course not."

"Voilà!" Richard opened the door to his bedroom, waving her inside. "The master bath is over here," he said, crossing behind her and opening another door that let into a water wonderland twice the size of Carol's living room. Her eyes widened. "There's a dressing room to the left. I'm sure I saw a couple of women's bathing suits some previous occupant left in the closet. The store labels are still attached, so it shouldn't be difficult to determine the size. Why don't you go ahead and change while I nip back downstairs and get the cognac?"

He left without waiting for an answer. Carol wandered into the master bath, goggling at its opulence. The bedroom was huge and beautiful as well, but there was a bed in there, naturally, and she didn't feel safe being that close to it. Was it Richard or herself she didn't trust? she wondered.

Carol didn't know what to call this place, but it certainly wasn't a bathroom. She counted herself lucky that her seventy-year-old house had two of those, one downstairs with a claw-footed tub, pedestal sink, and a commode that made ominous whistling noises when she flushed it; and another upstairs that had been modernized, complete with a fiberglass-and-plastic shower stall.

No plastic here. Everything in this room was slate-gray marble, smoked glass, or seasoned redwood. All the fixtures were gold-plated variations of swans, right down to the knobs on the cherry-red bidet. Double sinks, also cherry red, were set into a gray-tile vanity that ran the full length of the room, as did the mirror behind it. Across from that was an enormous shower enclosure with four spray heads, a pair each on either side of its marble tile walls. And then came the bathtub, a red monster with golden side rails that Carol at first thought was the whirlpool.

But no. That was in its own separate area behind a glass partition, sunken into the floor and surrounded by a padded knee-high wall paneled in tongue-and-groove redwood. She opened the glass door in the barrier and stepped inside, bending to dip her hand into the water. Then she immediately pulled it back out. Hot!

All right. So Richard didn't own all this. He was still rich enough to rent it for however long he planned to stay in Tithe, and that alone was enough to boggle Carol's mind. Everything around her was a joy to her highly trained eyes, a feast for her artistic soul. And yet something about it didn't suit her taste. There she was, amid such splendor, and the main thing she was thinking of was what a bitch it would be to clean.

Maybe that was at the root of her unsettled feelings for Richard. He was handsome and wealthy, led an undeniably luxurious existence; but something about both him and his lifestyle seemed too rich for her blood. Although Carol enjoyed beauty and luxury as much as the next woman, in her art as in her life, she had come to understand the pleasure simplicity had to offer.

Still, the place was a feast for the eyes. After a full minute of standing there with her mouth hanging open, however, she decided she'd better get a move on and find herself a suit before Richard returned.

The dressing room was to the left, as promised, as were two bathing suits on hangers at the far end of the closet, tags still dangling. Both were her size.

So this idea had just occurred to him? Sure it had.

She was there, the hot water was still tempting, and thus far Richard had behaved himself. So she decided to play along for the time being. That didn't mean she had to play it exactly his way, though. One of the suits was a two-piece with bandeau top and thong bottom. Absolutely not. The other, a more modestly cut pink-and-black maillot, wouldn't exactly hide everything she wanted hidden but would have to do. Carol closed the dressing-room door and put it on.

Richard knocked. "Find something?"

"Yes, thank you." As if he didn't know.

"Good, good. I'll just flip this switch and . . ." The muffled sound of bubbling water reached her through the closed door. Then he said, "Oops. Forgot the music."

Thinking to take advantage of his momentary absence, Carol came out of the dressing room and hurried over to the whirlpool. If she could just slip in before he got back, she could rob him of the opportunity to watch her prance around in front of him.

Carol sat down on the padded edge of the whirlpool, then swung her legs around and dangled them in the steaming, frothing water. When she stood up, the water came to the bottom of her buttocks. Evidently the air jets cooled the water slightly, because it wasn't quite as hot as she'd thought it would be. Still, it was hot enough that she didn't feel like sitting right down in it, either. So she waded around a bit, swiveling at the hips and letting her hands skim across the water's turbulent surface.

Music started playing, a soft piano concerto from concealed speakers. Her movements became a dance of sorts, timed to the lilting rhythm. She closed her eyes, so she didn't notice when the lights dimmed in the spa enclosure, bathing her in a rosy glow.

"Beautiful. Beyond any language I know. If I had your talent, I would sculpt you just as you are now, a water nymph at sensuous play in her secret pool."

Carol's eyes popped open and she spun around, her arms instinctively crossing over her breasts. Richard had changed into a brief swimsuit of his own. "Oh! I was just—"

"Relaxing," Richard interjected. He closed the glass door behind him. The wall was clear, but somehow closing that door completed the feeling of isolated intimacy. "You were relaxing and enjoying yourself, which is precisely why I invited you. I can already see your tension slipping away. And I have never seen the match for your loveliness."

Something in his voice made Carol lower her arms. She had a nice body, slim and taut, with small, pert breasts and well-rounded buttocks. If he wanted to look, let him look. It was only fair, after all. Because she suddenly realized why she was there. It wasn't for confirmation that a man other than Sean would find her attractive. It was to see if she could find another man attractive after Sean.

So while he studied her, Carol studied him. To begin with, he was about four inches shorter and a good forty pounds lighter than Sean, which gave him the lean, tough look of a panther compared to that of Sean's larger, more muscular tiger. Neither had any fat to spare. They both looked good in a swimsuit, something Carol deemed admirable for men in their late thirties. Like Sean, he appeared to have nice, trim buttocks. And as for the other asset his low-cut suit concealed . . . Well, her gladiator could rest easy on that score.

But not bad. Not bad at all. Richard's body looked just as Carol thought it would. She'd done enough nudes in her day to be as good at judging size and shape through fabric as he was. Of course, she had always stopped short of picturing his most masculine of male attributes, but now she allowed herself to do just that.

Good grief, Carol! Get a grip!

I'd love to.

Oh, no! She was starting to think like Bobbi!

"This does feel wonderful," she said, averting her eyes at last. "I'm glad I changed my mind."

"So am I. And it's even better all the way in."

She cleared her throat nervously and looked at him again, arching her eyebrows. "Excuse me?"

"The water," Richard explained with a knowing smile. "It's even better if you get all the way in."

"Oh. Yes. I was just trying to get used to the heat." Carol took his advice and sat down on the submerged fiberglass bench molded into the side of the tub. She sighed, closing her eyes and sinking in up to her chin. "God. This is great."

Leaving the glasses and crystal decanter of cognac he'd brought within easy reach on a shelf near her head, Richard stepped over the railing, joining her in the water. Unlike her, he took the plunge right away, slipping in right beside her. She jumped and opened her eyes when his thigh brushed hers. The coarse hair on his leg tickled.

"Come here often?" Carol asked, trying to sound glib and at ease. In reality she felt tight as a bowstring in spite of the hot water and soothing bubbles.

"As often as I can. It truly is the perfect cure for stress." He reached around her to pour them each a glass of cognac, handing her one and taking a sip at his own. "Have some. Part of the cure, you see."

The cognac was smooth as silk on her tongue, but she could feel its languid fire spread through her as it trickled down her throat, leaving her breathless for a moment. "Woosh! Enough of that!"

"Just one more sip. Dr. Richard's orders."

Carol complied. This time, it wasn't so much a fire she felt as a glowing ember, one that radiated outward from her chest. Her fingers and toes were beginning to tingle.

"Now," Richard said, taking her glass and setting it on the shelf beside his, "turn your back to me."

"What?"

"I'm going to massage that stiffness out of your neck."

"I don't think I—"

He tapped the tip of her nose lightly with his finger and said, "No thinking! Just relax." Putting his hands on her hips, Richard swiveled her around on the slick bench to the position he wanted. Then he started to massage her.

"Ouch!"

"Sorry. What were you doing all day? Lifting weights?"

"In a way," she murmured. She was tingling all over now, and couldn't decide whether she liked it or not. The pressure of his thumbs on the base of her neck did feel glorious, however, so she closed her eyes and leaned into it. "Bobbi and I poured a bunch of bronze mountain lions."

"Bobbi? Oh, that's right. Your charming albeit wary assistant." He paused in his ministrations for a moment. "How is work progressing on my sculpture by the way?"

Carol started to turn around. "It's—"

"No! Don't answer that." He went back to kneading her shoulder muscles. "I'm supposed to be helping you forget about business for a while. I'm sure the piece is coming along just fine."

"It's fine," Carol repeated in a lazy voice.

His cure was working. She leaned against the side of the whirlpool, totally relaxed. His strong fingers gliding along her spine, the heat, bubbles, and soft classical music, all combining with a pleasant blurriness provided by the cognac, transporting her into another world. She forgot work, Sean, even her uneasiness about Richard and whatever else he might be up to.

Then she felt his fingertips sliding along her sides at the edges of the swimsuit's plunging back. "Your skin is so soft and smooth," he said.

"Um . . ."

One of his hands pressed against the small of her back, moving in a small circle at the base of her spine. The other slipped beneath the elastic edge of her suit and wandered around her hip to cup the gentle swell of her stomach. His lips touched her shoulder, followed by the delicate nip of his teeth. Carol arched her back, moaning involuntarily.

Richard whispered, "That's better." The hand on her stomach dipped lower. "Relax. Just relax."

"Oh!" Carol sat up straight, trying to squirm away from him. It wasn't easy on the slippery fiberglass, especially with his hand inside her suit. "I feel faint!" she told him, finally managing to dislodge his hand. "I must be getting overheated."

"I know I am," Richard muttered under his breath. He curtly reminded himself of his goal for the evening and did his best to cool down. "You'd better sit on the edge for a while."

It sounded like a good idea to Carol. So did getting out of his reach. What didn't seem wise was to acknowledge what had just happened. She pulled herself out of the tub and perched on the padded edge, trying to smile.

"Whew! That takes some getting used to."

Richard moved closer to her dangling legs, a broad smile on his face. "I'm sure you'll get the hang of it. You seem like a natural to me."

"Maybe. But I don't have room for one of these at my place even if I could afford one." Perhaps if she ignored the whole thing, it would go away.

As you're trying to ignore your feelings for Sean?

That wasn't working, and apparently neither was this. "In for a penny, in for a pound," Richard said as he moved between her legs and started to massage her calves. "You'll thank me for this in the morning, darling. Your body will be singing my praises."

Carol wasn't sure what he meant by that. But her body was already singing, a confusing chorus of excitement and pleasure tempered by a healthy dose of purely feminine panic. He wasn't grabbing at her or trying to force himself on her, and yet she knew that if she didn't get the hell away from him, she was going to be his all the same.

Richard had abandoned her calves in favor of her thighs, stroking them in a long, languorous oval from her knees up the outside of her legs to her hips and back down again. Up. Down. Up. Down. The motion of his body as he rocked back and forth between her legs was deliberate and sexual, as was the way he was gradually widening the oval, allowing his fingertips to lightly caress the sensitive skin of her inner thighs with every stroke.

Suddenly, on the upstroke, his hands went to her buttocks and he pulled her off her perch, pressing her body against him as he lowered her slowly back into the water. He kissed her, lightly at first, then with more passion, parting her lips to touch her tongue with his own.

And then an amazing thing happened.

Richard let her go. Just like that. One second she was in his arms and the next she was sinking to a seat on the submerged bench, looking up at him. He seemed immensely pleased with himself.

"There we go," he said. "Completely cured and ready to sleep like a babe, awake refreshed, and fight another day." He reached for his glass of cognac, drained it, then turned and climbed from the whirlpool. "How do you feel?"

Frustrated. Relieved. A little bit like a discarded lump of modeling clay. Carol wasn't about to answer that question truthfully. "F-fantastic," she replied.

"I told you so." After grabbing a towel from a rack by the door, Richard started drying himself off. "Works wonders for me, though I don't have anyone to give me a massage, of course," he added with a sly smile. "Maybe next time."

"Uh . . . sure."

Carol sat there for a moment, then stood up and got out of the water. Her legs felt shaky. Richard came up behind her and wrapped her in a towel, giving her a quick hug.

"You'd better towel off, darling," he said. "I promised to have you home early, remember? There's a built-in blow dryer over near the shower for your hair."

She turned around and stared at him. "Richard . . ."

"Yes?"

There was an odd light in his eyes. Something akin to hope, she decided. He had done all a gentleman could do and now was secretly hoping she would take control of the situation. In fact she almost did, was afraid to think about what secrets her own eyes were revealing.

Instead she kissed him on the cheek and said, "Thanks."

"But of course! Hurry now, I won't have you making a liar of me." With that he left the spa enclosure and then the bathroom, closing that door behind him.

Bewildered, Carol toweled off and went to dry her hair. She was still bewildered when she met him downstairs awhile later—this time waiting until she had descended to the lower level to put on her high heels. Richard already had his black cashmere topcoat on and was holding her full-length down jacket for her. She slipped her arms in and buttoned it up.

It was only a half mile or so down the hillside into town, perhaps another half mile to Carol's house after that. Tithe was lit up like one big Christmas tree, twinkling beneath the starry December sky. A crèche glowed on the snow-covered front lawn of the church, while farther into town even the supermarket had decked its roof with a huge lighted Santa Claus, complete with festive red sleigh and prancing reindeer team.

The Naked Waitress was doing a booming business, Carol noticed, feeling a pang of guilt as they drove past. But why? Nothing had happened, not really. Not tonight.

"Just what do you have to take care of tomorrow?" Richard asked as he pulled up her snowpacked driveway.

Carol sighed. "Oodles. First thing in the morning, I have deliveries to make to the places that sell my work, so the last-minute shoppers dashing around can have something to snatch up, poor tortured souls."

"I beg your pardon! I happen to be a last-minute shopper myself and enjoy it very much, thank you."

"If you say so." She patted his shoulder and laughed. "After that, I'm going to finish up your sculpture. My helper is off and I'll have some peace and quiet for a change." Carol didn't bother telling him that she'd have to clean up her studio before she could even get to the piece to work on it. "And then in the afternoon I plan to run to see a few friends, play Santa, and wish them a merry Christmas."

Richard nodded. "But you'll be home Christmas Eve?"

"Sure." That panicky feeling returned. Of course he would want to see her tomorrow night. And she didn't think he'd still be playing the passive role or want to stop at a kiss, either. Still, she asked, "Why?"

"I thought I'd stop by for a while. I like to play Saint Nicholas too, you know." And collect a very special gift of his own, naturally. "That's part of what this poor tortured soul is going to be dashing around for tomorrow."

"You don't have to do that!"

"I want to."

Carol had planned to give him some homemade cookies. Suddenly, now that she knew he was getting her something, she had the sinking feeling cookies wouldn't be quite what he expected from her. Well, it was the thought that counted. He just thought in higher figures than she did.

He stopped the car and Carol leaned over to give him a quick kiss. That, too, was inadequate to his expectations, she was sure. "Nothing too expensive, okay?"

"By your standards or mine?" Richard asked, chuckling.

She wagged a warning finger at him, then got out of the car. "Good night."

"Good night. Pleasant dreams."

Richard waited until she got inside before he drove off, and Carol in turn waited until he was gone before she turned off the porch light and her own Christmas display.

What was she going to do? Something had to give, and soon, before her mind snapped. If she didn't deal with this guilty conscience of hers, she would never be able to really relax with Richard. As it was she didn't know if she even wanted what had almost happened between them tonight to happen Christmas Eve—his intention, she was sure.

All right. So there was still a part of her invested in Sean. That didn't mean she could transform herself into the kind of woman he wanted, which in turn meant the best thing to do was what she had failed to do so far. Break it off clean, as soon as possible.

It was quite a Christmas present to have to deliver, more hurtful than the divorce papers she'd given Frank and this time completely undeserved. But no less necessary. By this time tomorrow, Carol vowed, Sean would know for certain that it was over. And so would she.

~ 7 ~

Carol was up before dawn on Christmas Eve day, loading the back end of her ugly-but-functional four-wheel-drive van with merchandise. It was bitter cold out, but she was bundled up and the work helped keep her warm. Each breath turned into a plume of vapor, swirling above her head to mix with an icy sort of mist that hung in the frigid air.

Sometime during the night a storm front had moved into the area, depositing an inch of new snow atop the two feet already on the ground. There wasn't enough to shovel, though, so she trudged along the well-worn paths around her house and studio, listening to it squeak beneath her boots. The sky looked ominous, a flat, even shade of gray. At the moment only a few puffy flakes came floating down, but something was brewing up in those clouds, Carol knew, from experience as well as the weather forecast. She hoped it would hold off until she was back safe from making her deliveries.

The morning would be a long one, with a lot of tricky driving through the mountain passes along her route, but at every shop in every town she hit along the way there would be a friendly, eager smile and a mug of something hot to welcome her. If things went right, there would also be some checks as well, at least from the places that worked on a consignment basis rather than buying outright. But the latter would have news of good sales, so with any luck at all her trip would be as fruitful as it was lengthy.

Her van was always a little slow to awaken on these cold mornings, as was she, so while it warmed up Carol did the same, over a steaming cup of tea in her kitchen.

It was a big room, the largest in the house, with lots of those metal cabinets that were so popular during the era in which the old place was constructed. Their white enamel surfaces had become cream-colored over the years, and some had chips around the edges of the doors, but they were still quite serviceable. The floor was done in white-and-black squares of linoleum tile, faded but in pretty good shape considering how many miles they had on them. All the countertops—yards and yards of countertops—were yellow, a color she had decided to repeat when she'd painted the walls and hung new curtains.

Carol supposed a complete remodeling was in order, but it would seem a waste somehow. Everything worked, and besides, she liked her kitchen. It was quaint, warm, and homey, did in fact remind her of the one in the house where she grew up. Her parents had long since left

Denver in favor of Arizona, where their new home had all the modern conveniences, so her mother naturally failed to see the attraction. But then, that applied to everything Carol had done for the past ten years.

She shouldn't have become a bookkeeper. She shouldn't have *stopped* being a bookkeeper. Marrying Frank was a mistake, but divorcing him was even worse. The house was a wreck, Tithe was too cold, and what was she trying to prove with this artist stuff, anyway? And no children yet?

"You're in your thirties now, Carol. Wake up!"

Although she loved her mother and father dearly, Carol wasn't too torn up that they had decided to spend Christmas in Hawaii this year. Not that they would have come to Tithe in any case. Mr. Applegate didn't mind snow all that much but his wife abhorred it; unless it was absolutely necessary, their last visit to Tithe would be just that, at least in wintertime. Sunny beaches were fine with Carol, but not at Christmas, and she was much too busy to accept their invitation to join them anyway. So her mother would just have to wait until the spring thaw to pester her face to face.

After filling a vacuum bottle with more hot tea, Carol bundled back up and trudged out to her van, which was running nicely now. She wished she could say the same for herself.

Her decision to finally break the news to Sean was supposed to have quieted her nerves, but it had done just the opposite. To top it off, she'd awakened this morning with the imaginary sensation of Richard's hands upon her skin, a feeling she couldn't quite shake and wasn't sure she liked.

It seemed, therefore, that another decision was imminent. Richard wanted her and obviously meant to have her, but Carol no longer thought she wanted to be had. For all his wealth, charm, and carefully polished sexuality, he was and would remain a wolf in executive clothing.

Between the pressure of Sean's serious intentions and Richard's desire to use her and throw her away, there had to be some middle ground. What she needed to do, Carol now realized, was get rid of both of them so she could find it.

Deal with business, then Sean, then Richard. It was going to be a busy day. And from the look of the sky, she had better get on with it.

8

"Brr!" Jack came through the back door of The Naked Waitress stomping his feet and blowing on his hands. "Cold out there today. Betsy tried to turn around and go home on me three times on the way here. I think she figures we're in for a nasty one."

"According to the weatherman, she's right," Sean said. "Winter storm warning for the entire front range. Snow and plenty of it. I hope you brought her galoshes."

Betsy was Jack's pack mule. She had hauled plenty of ore and equipment in her day, but was now more of a pet. Jack often rode her into town. In fact he had a hard time keeping her at home. All the places Jack frequented kept some oats on hand for her to munch on while he was inside doing whatever it was he had to do. Since he spent so much time at the pub, Sean had even built a small shed out back so the mule would stay warm and dry when the weather was bad.

It wasn't too bad yet, just cold and some snow flurries, but it was predicted to get much, much worse by nightfall, and Betsy evidently hadn't thought a few oats were worth it.

While Jack was taking off his coat, Sean poured them both some coffee and took it to a table near the window where they usually ate breakfast. Actually, the pub didn't really open until ten, and by mutual agreement Sean didn't compete with the café down the street for Tithe's breakfast trade. They didn't serve hamburgers and fries, he didn't serve bacon and eggs.

But on any given morning Jack was likely to show up for some coffee and one of Sean's famous bran muffins. Since the pub's front doors were still bolted and Sean made it clear they were just sharing a friendly breakfast, it was the one thing Jack didn't insist on paying for. He was sitting at the table sipping coffee when Sean got back from the kitchen.

"Muffin?" Sean asked, putting a plateful between them and taking a seat himself.

"Don't mind if I do," Jack replied. "I love these things to death."

"I've been told I have a heavy hand with the bran."

Jack waved the complaint aside. "They just take getting used to. Some people don't know how to enjoy a good shit, that's all."

"It's my grandmother's recipe, and she does place a high value on keeping regular."

"Smart woman." Jack took a bite of his muffin, chewed thoughtfully, and washed it down with some coffee. "I have some news, but I'm not sure I want to tell."

"If it's about Carol going home with Palance last night," Sean said with a deep sigh, "I already know."

For a man who hadn't wanted to say anything, Jack looked pretty disappointed. "Damn bunch of snoops."

"As their titular head, you should know."

"Their what?" Jack asked, glaring at him.

"Unofficial leader. You had to snoop to find out what Carol was up to yourself, didn't you?"

Jack wasn't offended in the slightest. "Sure. But other than play pool and scratch around in the dirt, that's about all I have to do anymore. It's my job, you might say, and I don't like amateurs poaching on my territory."

"It wasn't an amateur," Sean assured him. "Old Mike stopped by for a beer on his way home after his shift at the condo gates. Next to you, he's the best."

"Well, that's okay then."

Sean didn't think so. He was starting to wonder if anything would ever be okay again. "Mike said they were only there for an hour or so. I'm probably getting myself worked up over nothing."

"Nothing! Son, the best I ever had in my life only took fifteen minutes."

"Fifteen minutes?" Sean shook his head and smiled in spite of all he had on his mind. "Now I know why no woman ever tried to marry you."

"I'll let that slide," Jack said irritably, "because there's a point to be made here. He took her to a fancy restaurant, probably got her tipsy, then got her to go home with him. What do you think they did for that hour? Play tiddledywinks?"

"You really know how to cheer a guy up, Jack."

"I'm sorry. But we're pals, right?" Sean nodded. "So who better to give you a kick in the butt? Unless you do something quick, you're going to lose that girl, Sean."

"I'm working on it."

"Well, work harder!"

"Not much to be done at the moment," Sean said. "I saw that van of hers chugging up the pass early this morning. That means she's off delivering artwork, probably won't be back till this afternoon." Then he smiled. "But I think I may have gotten my first break. Not long after I saw her heading up the mountain, I saw Palance's car heading down. He must have important business in Denver."

Jack looked out at the angry sky. "*Real* important. Damn fool thing to do with a storm like this coming."

"Yes," Sean agreed. "Isn't it, though."

9

Richard's Porsche could go from zero to sixty in seven seconds, with a top speed of over one hundred forty miles an hour. It had soft leather upholstery, a stereo that made it seem as if the Boston Philharmonic were sitting right behind him, and enough gauges, dials, and gadgets to keep an engineer's nose in the owner's manual for a week.

But in the kind of weather he was running into, it was little more than a forty-thousand-dollar sled.

The trip down out of the mountains had been a breeze, so easy in fact that he scoffed at the reports coming over the radio. Whatever this Albuquerque low was that all the weather people were worried about didn't seem bad at all. While the sky was certainly bleak and snow most definitely falling, the road crews weren't having any trouble keeping the roads scraped and sanded.

As he emerged from the foothills outside of Denver, however, Richard started to get the feeling he was in over his head. Snow was falling at an incredible rate, all but overloading his windshield wipers. The strong winds sweeping the area didn't help matters, except that so far they were blowing all that snow off the roads before it could stick.

But it had to go somewhere. Every sign was plastered with the stuff, causing him to miss his exit ramp.

Once back on track, he divided his time between reading the explicit directions Stevens had written down for him and avoiding idiots who were driving as if this were a fine spring day instead of a snowstorm. Whereas they didn't seem to have any other purpose than to motor around bashing into each other, Richard knew exactly where he wanted to go, what he had to buy, and whom he needed to speak with to get it.

The frustration of it all was unbearable. By the time he arrived at his destination, he had used more blistering profanity in two hours than he had in his entire life.

Stepping into the little clock shop was like entering another world in comparison to the urban chaos outside. He had to wait to see the man who handled special items such as the one he had driven all this way for, but Richard didn't mind. He strolled around, listening to the quiet ticking of all the timepieces. As luck would have it, he even found a gift for Stevens, an intricately engraved gold pocket watch a man of his punctuality was sure to prize.

When he at last left the shop with his purchases, Richard found that the weather hadn't improved a bit. It seemed impossible, but snow was coming down even harder than before. The streets were covered now, making traction an impish thing that was there one second, gone the next. And the city still hadn't run out of idiots.

Victims of lunch-rush traffic were everywhere, their cars scattered higgledy-piggledy, in ditches; half buried in huge drifts the overworked snowplows had pushed to the sides of the road; or simply abandoned wherever they had ceased to move forward. The highways were better, but a semitrailer truck had jackknifed across the westbound lanes of I-70, making it necessary to form a single-lane detour around it that held Richard fuming for the better part of an hour.

During that time he listened to the radio, learning a couple of things he really didn't want to know. The first was that an Albuquerque low could be capricious as well as fierce, blanketing one place while leaving another without a flake. While it made his decision to ignore the seemingly false reports earlier more understandable, it also made him feel like an uneducated fool for driving blithely on.

But the second thing he learned made him feel far worse. From all reports—which he now took as gospel—the storm was going to be his constant companion all the way back to Tithe. Instead of driving out of it, it was going to be as if he were towing it up into the mountains with him.

Providing he got that far. Something called a chain law was in effect for all mountain passes. The Porsche had good tires, but by the way it was already slipping around he didn't think the authorities were going to consider them adequate for the conditions. The other options were tire chains or a four-wheel-drive vehicle. What with the worst storm to hit these parts in years going on, at one o'clock in the afternoon on the day before Christmas, Richard didn't like his chances for acquiring either one.

At any other time, he would have turned around and checked into the best hotel he could find. Only two thoughts made him drive on through the blowing snow: Carol, waiting for him by a cozy fire; and the gaily gift-wrapped box safe beside him in the passenger seat. No man, and certainly no storm, was going to stop Richard Palance from turning his dreams into reality.

10

Sean reached across the grill to flip a row of hamburger patties, moving with practiced ease from left to right, then dropping down to the next row and repeating the process in the opposite direction. In one row, each received a measure of grilled onions on top, the other he left plain. After a moment, he deftly placed the top of a toasted bun on all the sizzling patties, slipped his spatula beneath them, and lifted them one by one onto the bottoms of the buns, and from there to plates.

He smiled, glad to know he hadn't lost his touch. The pub was closed tomorrow and would close early this evening too, so Sean had given his regular cook and one of the two waitresses some extra time off, figuring he could manage just fine. After all, he'd run the place by himself for the first couple of years.

What he'd forgotten about was that Tithe had grown since then, and his business along with it. He also hadn't figured many people would be out and about, especially with the weather deteriorating by the hour. He'd figured wrong.

After a mad rush that had kept him hopping

since noon, the orders were finally tapering off. Sean added garnish to the plates and put them on the ledge of the pass-through window, along with several orders of fries, then sat down on a nearby stool to catch his breath. He glanced at his watch, eyes widening at the time. Three o'clock!

Maureen came by and collected the food. She didn't call out any orders. Sean sat there, silently blessing her and trying to remember all the things he had to do.

Pick up Carol's present. Call his father and tell him to tell the rest of the O'Phaelan brood that the roads might very well be closed tomorrow, and that since that wouldn't stop the reckless louts for them to be very careful on their way there tomorrow. Ask his mother very sweetly not to bring the dogs along, and make her promise not to worry if he's a bit late for the Christmas party. If it didn't snow so hard they'd have to dig their way down to the The Naked Waitress even to have a party.

Last but very far from least, call his friend at Highland Hawk and make sure he could still rent a snowmobile. If the storm hit Tithe as hard as it was now hitting Denver, a tracked all-terrain vehicle might very well be the only thing that could get down the mountain later. And getting down was the one thing he absolutely had to do.

As Sean sat pondering all these things, something very soft and warm pressed against his back. "Trouble, Sean?"

"Yes," he replied. "You. What do you want, Maureen?"

She moved around him, rubbing her large, full breasts against him as she went. "Don't be like that. You know what they say. The fastest way to get over a broken heart is get it next to another one as soon as you can."

"In the first place, I've never heard that particular saying, and in the second, I don't have a broken heart." At least not yet, he added silently.

Maureen either didn't believe him or didn't care. She continued to apply her remedy, by wrapping her arms around him and practically smothering him in her ample bosom.

"Mmph!"

"Is that a yes or a no?" the waitress asked.

Sean dislodged himself and put her at arm's length. "It's your boss asking you how well you like your job," he replied. "For the last time, Maureen, I'm not interested."

"How can you make a fool of yourself over that little slip of a girl when you have a real woman who's just aching to have a man like you inside . . . I mean in her life?"

She stuck her lower lip out in a pout. Maureen was quite a woman, no doubt about it. With her long black hair, eyes even greener than his own, and a body that put many a centerfold to shame, she had every reason to ask a man why he wasn't interested in her, Sean supposed. There was a time when Maureen would have been the one beating him off with a stick.

But that was before he'd lost his heart. True, Carol was stepping on it. And maybe he was making a fool of himself. No amount of pain, however, would change the fact that he loved her. Sean was willing to do anything and everything he could to get her back.

"That's my concern," he told Maureen sternly. "Your concern is those customers out there. Go tend to them."

"They're fine." She inched closer to him, running the tip of her tongue around her full red lips. "I'd rather service you."

Sean sighed and looked up at the ceiling. "For crying out loud! What am I going to do with you?"

"Well," she replied, coming closer still and putting her arm around him, "like I said, the rush is over and I've made everybody happy. Except you. We could go upstairs and . . ."

Maureen whispered a suggestion in his ear. Sean's eyebrows shot up. It wasn't that her imagination surprised him; in fact he wasn't even listening. The shock on his face was caused by something else entirely.

"I dropped by to give you your Christmas present," Carol said from the kitchen doorway. "But from the looks of things, I'll have to stand in line."

11

Carol wasn't jealous. After all, she hadn't seen Sean in almost two weeks, had gone hot-tubbing with another man last night, and was now planning on telling this one she was breaking up with him. What possible reason did she have to think of Sean as hers, when she was doing everything she could not to think of herself as his?

No, she wasn't jealous. It was simply that she had never liked Maureen. That's why she wanted to grab her by her enormous boobs and throw her out into the snow.

Some modicum of the confused anger Carol was feeling must have shown in her eyes, for as she stepped into the kitchen, Maureen started sidling toward the door.

"Some of your customers would like their checks," Carol said. As the other woman edged past, she added in a low voice, "So get your fat ass out there and leave Sean alone."

Maureen flounced off. Carol turned to Sean. He was still sitting there with a stunned expression on his face.

"Carol! I—"

"Save it." She shoved a gift-wrapped tin plate full of chocolate chip cookies under his nose. "Here's your present. And I hope you choke!"

Sean took the cookies from her and put them aside. "I thought I'd gotten used to your artistic temperament," he said in a carefully controlled tone. "But I guess I was wrong. Two weeks, Carol! If anyone has the right to be angry it's me, and by God you better believe I am!"

"Oh, really? Is that what you were doing? Working off your anger with Miss Knockers?" This wasn't at all how it was supposed to go. She'd come here to tell him they were through, not fight about him fooling around with Maureen. "Not that I really give a damn. Just don't try to tell me how lonely you've been without me, that's all."

"And don't you dare try to blame me for our troubles," Sean told her. "You know Maureen has the hots for me, and you know I've never done a thing to encourage her. The only reason she was putting the moves on me is that she thinks I'm unclaimed territory now. And with the way you've been acting lately who can blame her?"

"You don't own me!"

"I never said I did!" Sean exclaimed. Forcing himself to remain calm, he reached out and took her hand. "But I did think we had an understanding. I have been lonely. And confused. How am I supposed to feel when the only woman in my life suddenly starts avoiding me? Did you think it wouldn't hurt when I started getting secondhand reports of your antics with Palance? Don't you think you owe me an explanation at the very least?"

She turned away from his intense gaze. Why did his eyes have to be so damned green? "I'm sorry. You're right. You do deserve an explanation. But as far as Richard is concerned, there's really nothing to tell."

"Nothing!"

"It's true! Richard is a client. We've been out to dinner a few times and . . ." Carol trailed off. Why was she beating around the bush like this?

Sean stood up. He still held her hand. With his other he touched her softly on the cheek, making her look at him again. "And you went home with him last night."

"Sometimes I hate this town," she muttered. "Yes, I went home with him last night. I was tired and sore from pouring castings all day and he kindly offered to let me use his whirlpool bath. After that he took me home." Carol frowned, mad at him for being so infuriatingly gentle with her and at herself for allowing it to sway her from her intended mission. "But this really isn't any of your business. The reason I'm here—"

"None of my business?" Sean interrupted. "We were lovers, Carol. As far as I'm concerned we still are. If you're sleeping with another man I have a right to know."

"I am not sleeping with Richard Palance!"

Someone started clapping. They both turned to the kitchen door. "Hallelujah!" Jack cried.

"Jack Bensen!" Carol started toward him. "If you're not out of my sight in two seconds, so help me . . ."

"Whoops! I think I'd better go check on Betsy. Bye!"

He scrambled for the nearest exit, moving incredibly well for a man his age. Sean chuckled, but when Carol turned on him he sobered instantly.

"Perhaps we'd better continue this discussion in less public surroundings," he suggested, putting a hand on her shoulder and leading her toward the stairway to his rooms above the pub. "Maureen! I'm taking a break."

Maureen acknowledged him, then turned away, scowling.

Carol didn't want to go upstairs with him. All day long she'd been rehearsing what she would say, practicing staying cool and logical about the whole thing. When she arrived at the pub, she had felt fully prepared, ready for any argument. But how quickly all that had flown out the window the moment she saw him with Maureen!

She hadn't counted on the way it would make her feel to see Sean again. No amount of advance planning could have prepared her for the surge of emotion that hit her when they stepped into his apartment. Carol had missed this place. And yes, dammit, she'd missed him too.

This was where it had all started, at least in her eyes, on that night she'd needed to talk to someone so badly. Behind that door on the other side of the living room was the bed where they first made love. They had spent quite a few Sundays on his couch too, reading the papers, sharing one of the omelettes he fixed so well, or playing love games late into the afternoon.

Suddenly Carol felt like crying. She wanted to be there and yet wanted to run. The memories flowing over her made her pulse race, but so did the fear of what it would take to return to his warm embrace. Love. Commitment. Marriage.

No. Never again. "Sean . . ."

"How about a nice, hot cup of tea?" he asked.

Another memory. The night she'd come looking to drown her sorrows and bitch about Frank, that was what he offered her. A strong, hot cup of tea with a dollop of Irish whiskey. And a broad shoulder to cry on. She wanted both right now, but couldn't risk either one. That was how she'd gotten into this muddle in the first place.

"No, thank you," Carol replied. "I have something to tell you, Sean, and I wish you'd just let me say it."

"I don't suppose it's merry Christmas?"

"Dammit! Would you be serious?"

Sean took a seat on the couch with a heavy sigh. "I thought that's why you took your leave of absence in the first place. Because you thought I was *too* serious."

"It is . . . I mean it was . . . Oh, hell!" Carol didn't dare sit down next to him, so she settled for walking around the room. "I'm confused, okay? I don't own you, either, and yet it pissed me off to see Maureen slobbering all over you."

"Then I guess I'm allowed to say I'm relieved you haven't gone to bed with Palance." Relieved was hardly the word for how he felt about that.

"I don't know why I told you that, either."

Sean leaned forward and rested his chin in his hands, watching her aimless pacing. She was so lovely. The way her gray slacks hugged her long legs and firm derriere; the soft swell of her breasts beneath her teal sweater; her pale-blond hair, glistening as she moved to look out the window at the snow coming down outside.

"You told me because you wanted me to know," Sean said.

Carol glanced at him. "Why should I?"

"Maybe you were feeling guilty."

"Same question. Why should I feel guilty?"

Sean got up and joined her at the window. What he wanted to do was scoop her into his arms and take her to bed, reestablish what Jack had so coarsely referred to as his claim on her. But she wasn't the only one who was confused. Carol was not the sort of woman a man could lay claim to in that manner. She had to be won, slowly and with tenderness, which was precisely what Sean thought he'd done before all this happened. So what now?

"Look, Carol," he began uncertainly, "I accepted your excuse that you were too busy to see me, but I knew that the real reason was that something was troubling you. You needed some space and I was happy to give it to you. Well, not happy, but I know we all have to have breathing room now and again. The last thing I expected you to do was to go right out and fill that space with another man."

"I didn't!" she objected. "He came in to order a special piece done and asked me out to dinner. I didn't plan it. It just . . . it just happened."

"And kept on happening."

Carol hadn't figured on it being this tough. She had already hurt him, could see his pain etched into the craggy lines of his handsome face. She wanted to touch him, run her fingers though his auburn hair, and kiss that pain away. Her arms ached to be around him. He was much too close.

"Stop looking at me like that!" She started wandering around again, while Sean leaned against the wall by the window, watching her. "I didn't do anything wrong!"

"Who are you trying to convince? Me?" He laughed bitterly. "I'm the one who went around for two weeks with egg on his face, remember? From where I stand you did plenty wrong. You're the only one in town who doesn't see it that way."

"Screw them! And screw you too!" she cried.

"Enough!" Sean pushed himself away from

the wall and had her by the arms before she could move an inch. "I'd like to scream and yell at you too, you know," he told her in a soft, menacing tone. "But it occurs to me that's what you were hoping I'd do, so you'd have an excuse to blame me for something rather than face up to the demon that's been plaguing you ever since you divorced Frank."

"The only demon after me is you!"

"Hush! You've had your say, now it's my turn. I'd also like to go find Richard Palance and rip his head off, but unlike him—and you—I have a certain regard for the way people should treat each other. Don't tell me you haven't done anything wrong, I can damn well see the guilt in your eyes. And stop pretending you don't know what I'm talking about. I can see that in your eyes as well."

Sean had never treated her this way before. It scared her, not because she was afraid he'd harm her, but for the simple fact that Carol had come to see him as a friend as well as a lover. His anger made her realize both would be gone from her life, and she didn't think she could deal with such a loss. Her confusion was now totally mind-numbing.

"What?" she asked quietly. "What else do you see in my eyes?"

"The same thing that frightens you in mine."

Although he could tell the last thing she needed at the moment was more pressure, Sean could no longer help himself. He wrapped his arms around her and held on tight, reveling in the feel of her body so close to his.

Carol didn't struggle. His arms felt too good around her. She tilted her head to look up at him, knowing what he was about to do and wanting it, willing it to happen. As he lowered his lips to hers, she intertwined her fingers in his hair, deepening the kiss. It had been only days since their last kiss, but it seemed like years, and suddenly the only thing Carol wanted was to make up for lost time.

Their tongues met, melding together, as did their moans of satisfaction and need. She felt his hands slip beneath her sweater, rubbing her back, then her sides. What had she been thinking of? This was the only man she wanted to touch her. In comparison Richard was like a machine, efficient, knowing all the right places but with a calculating detachment that left her feeling hollow inside afterward. For Sean, her nipples stood at attention, awaiting his touch, the sweet, gentle touch of a man who loved her, cared for her, took joy in her pleasure as well as his own.

Sean didn't disappoint her. Her breasts, twin points of heat against his palms, made him groan with desire for her. She pulled his shirttails free of his jeans, yearning to feel his bare skin. His back felt so warm, so solid beneath her fingertips. Leaning heavily on him, trapping his hands between them, Carol rubbed herself against him, feeling the pulsing strength of his manhood. She thought of him entering her, again and again, letting a dizzy wave of anticipation wash over her.

This had to be what she wanted. No panic gripped her now. How could she have been such a blind, stupid fool?

Carol pulled away from him, gazing into those amazing green eyes of his. He was right. She could see the love in them, and in a way it still frightened her. But as always, it was impossible to be afraid in his strong arms.

"Sean, let's—"

The brisk knock on his door interrupted her —and broke the spell that had woven itself around them both. "Excuse the interruption," Maureen called out, not sounding the least bit apologetic. "But there's a guy downstairs who needs to talk to you, Sean. Said he knows he's early, but that it couldn't be helped."

"Damn!" Sean exclaimed softly. "I'm sorry. It's my fault. I should've known better than to start this with a room full of people downstairs." He took his hands from beneath her sweater, blowing out a deep, frustrated breath.

Carol was also breathing heavily. She disentangled herself from his shirt and took a step back from him, fighting to get a grip on her emotions. "No, we're both at fault," she assured him. "It takes two, after all."

Exactly. She had been about to ask him to take her to bed, when she should have known the idea was doomed from the start. Doomed for more than one reason. Maybe a part of her *did* know they would be interrupted. Was she perhaps even counting on it?

Her confusion came back full force, and suddenly she was cursing herself for being so weak. Carol turned away from him, not wanting him to see her face. He was too good at figuring out what was going on inside her.

"Carol, what's the matter?" Sean moved around her, trying to get her to look at him. "It's all right. As soon as I close up we can—"

"No! I have work to do and . . . I'm sorry, Sean. This shouldn't have happened at all."

She started toward the door. He beat her there, blocking her way. "I'm not letting you run away again."

"Dammit!" Pushing tears from her eyes with the back of her hand, she told him, "You have to! I'm still confused. I need more time to work this out, Sean. I . . . I'm sorry."

Carol brushed past him and opened the door. She knew he could easily have stopped her, wasn't sure why he didn't, and that, too, confused her. Practically bowling Maureen over on her way, she took the stairs two at a time, grabbed her coat from the rack by the front entrance, and ran out into the snow, leaving Sean standing in his apartment.

"Poor timing, huh?" Maureen asked him.

Sean glared at her. "Send the guy up," he said, then shut the door in her face. He glanced at his watch.

Carol wanted time? Fine. She had about four and a half hours. Then she was going to come face to face with her personal demon whether she wanted to or not.

12

The snow had tapered off some, but Stevens knew that was a temporary affair. From where he stood by the window he could see Mr. Palance's condominium and the place where he'd been parking his Porsche. The condo windows were all dark and the parking slot covered with six inches of fresh, powdery snow that the maintenance man hadn't gotten to with his little tractor yet.

There hadn't been much sun to speak of all day and now, with nightfall fast approaching, it was positively gloomy outside. Or would have been, except for the festive Christmas lights coming on all over the place. They didn't do much to improve Stevens's mood. He was worried.

"Damn the man for his obstinacy!"

Stevens would have been glad to make the run to Denver for him, had in fact practically begged to do just that again this morning when Richard took off. His chances of making it there and back through a storm that was reportedly crushing the city wouldn't have been any better, of course. That was the point. *He* wasn't obsessed with the Applegate woman. At the first sign of trouble, he would have parked that utterly useless sports car and walked to the closest inn.

But of course, Richard refused to change his mind, as Stevens had known he would; just as he knew that his employer wouldn't hear of admitting defeat. Goodness no. Without question, Mr. Richard Palance was somewhere out on those treacherous mountain passes this very minute, slogging along through the storm, bound and determined to make his Christmas Eve tryst. Or die in the effort.

It wasn't such a melodramatic idea. All day long the television stations had interrupted their regular programming to give updates on the storm's steady march, along with scenes of its fury. One missed corner on a winding mountain road in a blizzard and . . .

Suddenly Stevens smiled. But of course! The Highway Patrol wouldn't allow him to proceed in a vehicle so obviously ill equipped for such conditions! Why, they had undoubtedly turned him back long ago. And a downed phone line would explain why he hadn't called.

Turning away from the window, Stevens grabbed the telephone receiver and lifted it to his ear. No dial tone. He put it back in its cradle with a deep sigh of relief and sank into a nearby chair.

Thank heaven for the authorities! Perhaps he couldn't prevent Palance from killing himself over a planned sexual encounter, but they could. And had, Stevens was now certain. If not, they surely would, once Richard got stuck, which he most likely already was. Stevens hoped, with a vindictiveness totally uncharacteristic for him, that the arrogant bastard got a good chilling down while he waited for rescue.

His mind wasn't totally at rest, but he did feel better at having worked out the most logical sequence of events. Richard was right; he'd been entirely too much the mother hen lately. And by God, he could indeed use some relaxation.

What was it Richard had said? Ah, yes. The pub had a fine bitter ale and pocket billiard tables. What was the use of staying home by a phone that might very well be out for days, worrying needlessly?

Stevens got up and went to the closet, pulling out the big parka he'd purchased on that awful trip to Alaska last year. Then as now, it made him look unbearably silly, but kept him warm as toast. He found the hat he'd stuffed into one pocket, his leather gloves in the other, then grabbed a pair of rubbers from the closet floor and put everything on.

He felt like an ass, but the fresh air would clear out the cobwebs, and the thought of a few pints of bitter ale was suddenly very appealing. Would the pub be open? No way of checking, unless he asked someone along the way.

"So, out the door with you!" he told himself. "After all, it's Christmas Eve!"

13

Carol consulted the drawing she had made from Richard's original rough sketch. Much more detailed as well as skilled, hers also had measurements in scale written on it and some strategic spots enlarged at the side to show detail. She snipped off a length of stainless steel wire, secured it in the jeweler's clamp sitting on her workbench, then moved the clamp until one end of the wire touched the almost completed sculpture at just the right spot. Working carefully amid the maze of wires already in place, she fluxed the joint, heated it with her torch until it glowed, then quickly applied a small amount of silver solder. Done.

The sculpture looked quite delicate, but in fact she could have bounced it on the floor without damaging it if she'd cared to. She didn't. What she did was pick it up and carry it over to the deep plastic sink at the back of the studio, where she washed this final joint with a solution of baking soda and water, then rinsed and dried it. Like the hundred or so other carefully made joints, this one was shiny and perfect.

All that was left was to attach the creation to

its base, a big free-formed lump of bronze that looked solid but actually had a cavity in the underside to reduce weight. It was still pretty heavy, so rather than carry it to her bench, Carol wheeled her torch and gas cylinder over to it instead. There were three attaching points cast into the bronze, placed in such a way that she didn't need to make them pretty, but she did anyway.

"There," she said, and stood back to have a good look.

She had taken quite a few liberties with Richard's design. It was still his concept, but now it flowed, almost sang. Almost. From certain angles it still looked like a ball of barbed wire with feet, or rather one big foot of gnarly bronze. The idea was his, the money was his, and soon the sculpture itself would be his, but the talent and final effect of the piece would always be hers.

That was why she'd worked so hard to make it the best it could be—in two weeks at that. To a certain extent she had failed, but she didn't let it bother her too much. An artist who did not wish to starve and suffer was often called upon to prostitute that art. Later on in her career she could hold the line against the tyrannical dollar; at the moment she needed those dollars or she wouldn't even have a career. As Richard would say, *C'est la vie.*

All Carol could say was that he'd damn well better like the stupid thing, because if he didn't, she was in just the right mood to tell him to shove it up his ass.

Confused was no longer an adequate description of her emotional state. At wit's end was more like it, with a healthy dose of rage lying just below the surface, ready to spring out and vent itself at any moment. The problem was, she didn't know whom she was mad at.

Yourself?

Yes, for one. But the reason was vague, hiding in the shadows of her mind. Since it was the least focused anger of all, Carol couldn't do anything about it. So she had to turn to other sources for an answer.

Sean. She was furious with him for loving her and for making her realize she loved him too. Strange, possibly even deranged, considering that being in love was supposed to make one happy, not angry. But that was how she felt and she had her reasons, heaven knew.

Frank. The jerk! Carol couldn't blame him for all her troubles. It was, after all, her fault that she had taken his abuse of their love and turned it into the fear she had of that emotion today. But she hadn't been able to take it in her stride, mainly because he hadn't let her. That made him enemy number one in her book. If he did show up this year, Carol hoped there was someone around to hide the ax.

Richard? She didn't hate him. But she didn't like him very much, either. Last night she had come within a breath of having sex with him. Not making love, just having sex, pure carnal knowledge of one another. There was a difference in her opinion, but Richard was very, very good at making that difference look inconsequential. That was why she disliked him. He was offering her a gold-plated, diamond-encrusted alternative to Sean that seemed like her only way out.

Which brought her back around the vicious circle to herself again. Carol was mad at herself for even considering the possibility, but couldn't help wondering what Sean would have done earlier if she'd said she *had* slept with Richard last night. A lot of things, probably, including some pretty harsh language. And afterward, he might have done what she had tried to do in the first place. Break up.

Carol was even less sure that that was what she wanted to happen now than she had been before. Seeing Sean had been a big mistake, had robbed her of what little certainty she'd had. What she did know was that anything was better than the mental torture she was going through now. Ending the relationship wouldn't be easy on her, either, but at least the pressure would be gone.

Since she couldn't manage to say the words, maybe she could force him to say them. Not that she had any intention of taking Richard to bed. The only thing she was going to screw him on was the price of his sculpture. But he was going to stop by tonight, and without a doubt everyone in Tithe would know about it. Including Sean. All she had to do was tell a lie, one

Richard wasn't likely to refute, knowing his ego.

After taking one last look at the finished sculpture, Carol shrugged, put her tools away, and turned out the lights. It was dark outside now, and the view through the studio windows beckoned to her. She went into the house, got her coat, and stepped out onto her front porch.

She wasn't all that tired, surprising after the day she'd had so far. But she did enjoy the way the cold, clean air nipped at her cheeks and cleared her mind. As she stood there, gazing out at the lights of town spread across the horizon, something Carol had of course known all along came back to the front of her consciousness.

It was Christmas Eve. There was a fairy-tale quality to Tithe this night. Viewed through a noiseless downpour of glistening snowflakes, a hazy glow seemed to hang over their secluded valley, wrapping a halo around each twinkling light. The silence was profound, as if the storm heading in their direction wasn't just cutting them off from civilization, but transporting them out of time entirely.

And then, off in the distance, she could hear a band of hardy carolers singing the joys of the season. Their voices floated across the snow-covered hills, muted and sweet. Carol hummed along for a moment, then stopped, listening. Children were playing somewhere. Soon their mothers would call them in for the night. There would be hot chocolate by the fire, something festive to eat, and then it would be time for the little ones to hop into bed. Would their fathers read them a story while they pretended to go to sleep, as hers had?

This would certainly be a good night for a long winter's nap. Snow was still coming down in fits and starts, but when it did fall it didn't play around. The tracks of her van in the driveway were gone now, as were the paths she'd reshoveled upon returning home. From the looks of things, the reports were right. They were in for the kind of accumulation they usually escaped. It would be counted in feet, not inches.

A breeze started whipping up from the east. Carol shivered and went back inside. Her phone made a curious half-ring, then stopped. She stared at it, then took off her coat and went into the kitchen, having put herself in the mood for some hot chocolate. The milk was about to boil when the phone rang again, this time in earnest.

"Oh . . . just a second!"

She poured some cocoa into a cup, spilling it, then spilled the milk as well. After carrying the hot mug gingerly into the living room, she sat down in her comfy old wing backed chair and picked up the receiver.

"Hello?"

Static. Carol thought she could hear a voice, but not clearly enough to make out. Then the static went away so completely she thought the connection had been broken.

"Well, shit!"

"Don't cuss, dear."

"Mom!" Carol practically dropped her hot chocolate in her lap. She sat the mug on the table beside the phone and sat up straight. "I'm sorry, I couldn't hear you and then I thought the line went dead again. Did you try to call a few minutes ago?"

"No. I told you that old house would be a nuisance."

"You are calling from halfway around the world, Mom," she pointed out. "And there's a storm brewing here. We're getting a hell . . . I mean a heck of a lot of snow, and more is on the way."

"Well, you can't blame me for that, can you? I told you not to move into that frigid little hole. Your father and I spent the day on the beach."

Carol rolled her eyes. "Did I say I blamed you?" she asked, trying to hide her exasperation. "And I'm glad you and Dad are having a good time."

Silence. Then her mother sighed. "Well, we do miss you. A family should be together at Christmas. You're at least having some friends over?"

"Uh, someone is supposed to stop by later. If he can get up my driveway, that is," Carol replied. Quick, a change of subject. "How about you guys? What—"

"He? Oh, you must mean Sean. He's such a nice young man, Carol. By the way you went on about him in your last letter, I thought for sure we'd be hearing good news soon. You didn't do anything to mess this one up, did you?"

Had she written that much about Sean? Yes, she supposed she had, in part to get her mother off her back about dating again. Carol had the feeling there was more to this phone call than Christmas sentimentality.

"If you must know, Sean and I are . . . It's over."

Liar.

All right, so it was in the process of being over. She wasn't going to even try to explain that to her mother.

Another sigh. "So you did mess it up."

"Mother!"

"I can't help it, dear. You know I love you, but sometimes a mother has to tell her daughter she's being an idiot. Don't you want to be happy?"

"Of course I do, but—"

"Then why do you insist on tossing out every chance at happiness that comes your way?"

Carol gritted her teeth. "Frank wasn't a chance at happiness, Mom. He was a ticket to disaster."

"Then what about that sweet boy you dated for a while in college?" she asked, cheerfully ignoring Carol's sarcasm. "Billy Bell?"

"Peale. Bill Peale." Strange, she hadn't thought about him in years. "You can't throw that one in my face. Don't you remember? He was the one who left me."

Her mother continued without skipping a

beat. "And now Sean. This has to stop, Carol. Don't you think I know how difficult men can be? Your father and I have had our share of differences over the years, heaven knows! But we stuck it out. And neither of us would have it any other way. We love each other. That's why I pester you, dear; I want you to be as happy as we are."

It was true. Carol's mother and father were so very happy together, a fact her mother took great pride in reminding her of at every opportunity. Carol could practically see her sitting there, wringing her hands in despair at her daughter's plight.

"I know you want the best for me, Mom. It's just that I have a lot of trouble . . . It's very complicated. Maybe we'll talk about it some other time. I'm sure this call is costing you a fortune."

"You're worth every penny. I'd put your father on, but he strained his back at the beach today and had to take a muscle relaxant. Those things always put him right out."

"Is he okay?"

"He'll be fit as a fiddle come morning. Said to give you his love and that he'd call you tomorrow. You know he likes to find out if you're enjoying your presents and tell you about his. You did get our package, didn't you?"

"It's underneath the tree," Carol assured her. "You got mine before you left for Hawaii?"

"We did. And we love it." There was a pause. When Edna Applegate spoke again, she sounded a little weepy. "You know, you really are becoming quite an artist. That ballerina seems alive, ready to dance right off. I spoke to your Uncle Fred the other day, and he's so proud of you he could burst; proud of himself as well, naturally, for starting you out. I guess it was worth losing my dining-room table after all."

"Thanks, Mom." Carol felt weepy now too. "I'd better let you go. Merry Christmas!"

"Merry Christmas, honey. Just one more thing."

Of course. Carol leaned back in her chair. "Yes?"

"It's only because I love you so much that I hound you about this. You know that. But you're coming to that age when alarm bells are going to start ringing. You were a trial at times, enough to occasionally make me glad I couldn't conceive again, but you're also my biggest joy in life. I'm not telling you to dash right out and have a baby. I just want to be sure you're thinking about it."

"Okay."

"And think about this. Happiness doesn't just come to you; you have to work at it. Sometime, maybe one cold night very soon, the ghosts of every relationship you've ever walked away from might come back to haunt you. Sweet dreams."

There was a click on the line, then static. Carol sat there listening to it for a moment, eyes wide. At last she hung up the phone and slumped back into her chair.

Merry Christmas to you too, Mom.

Suddenly her gaily decorated living room seemed cold and empty. She got up and plugged in her Christmas tree, then went around the room lighting candles, hoping to recapture the spirit. There was a fire already laid in the fireplace, and she lit that too, then sat back down to sip at her hot chocolate. It wasn't hot anymore, and she'd forgotten to stir it, so lumps of cocoa floated on top.

Obviously, strange moods ran in her family. What was that last part all about? The ghosts of her relationships? Bizarre. And silly. Still, as she sat gazing into the hypnotic flames leaping in the fireplace, Carol got the uneasy feeling her mother had just delivered some kind of ominous warning.

Then she looked at her mug of hot chocolate and made a face. "Indigestion," she muttered. "That's all it is."

14

"Are you still serving?"

Maureen looked the stranger up and down. Not bad in a stuffy sort of way. Weird coat, though. "Sure am, handsome. As long as you don't want anything more complicated than a cold roast beef sandwich. The boss is out running errands so I'm pulling double duty. Triple, considering I'm the waitress too."

Stevens arched his eyebrows. "Not *the* waitress?"

"You mean the naked one? Joke's on you, pal." She pointed to the erotic wood carving above the bar. "That's the only pair you're going to see. Unless you get lucky," she added with a sly wink.

"Yes, well . . ."

He removed his coat and went to hang it up, then returned to the bar and sat down on one of the stools. There were plenty to choose from; only a handful of people were in the pub, including some old geezer playing billiards in back.

"What'll it be?" Maureen asked.

"As I've already eaten, I believe I'll have a pint of bitters, please."

She giggled. "You're cute. One ale, coming up."

Stevens watched as she drew him a tall glass of rich, brown ale, smiling in anticipation. His little walk had been pleasant, if a tad chilly, but had left him with a powerful thirst. As soon as the large-breasted woman set his glass in front of him, he lifted it and drained a third of it immediately. It was, as Richard had said, very fine.

"Oh, my! That is good! And not frozen solid like most establishments in this country serve."

"Sean knows his brews," Maureen said.

As long as he was there, Stevens supposed he should find out what Richard's rival for the Applegate woman's affections was up to this evening. "So Mr. O'Phaelan left you here to fend for yourself, did he?"

"He had some shopping to do, stuff like that. He'll be back in about an hour to close up."

"I see." He finished his ale. "May I have another?"

"You may," she replied, grinning at him. "Better watch it, though. This stuff is potent."

Stevens shrugged. "No harm. I'm afoot."

He quaffed the second as quickly as he had the first, and found that he was actually starting to relax. Again, Richard had been correct. Hard work was something Stevens enjoyed, but without a bit of fun to balance it out, one could easily become obsessed.

Of course, for a man like him, one obsession was easily replaced with another. He studied the barmaid. She was very striking, and the ale was having a very curious effect on his nervous system.

After ordering a third glass, he waited until she placed it in front of him, then returned her wink from earlier. "I know where I'd be if I were your employer. Out buying you a present. Or have you been a naughty girl?"

Maureen leaned on the bar. "If there's anyone naughty around here, it's you." She batted her eyelashes at him coquettishly. "A thirsty stranger in town and on foot. Where did you come from, handsome?"

"The condominium complex up the hill." He extended his hand. "The name's Stevens. I'm personal secretary to Mr. Richard Palance."

"Really?" Maureen knew most people in town hated the man. The only thing that bothered her about the way he'd taken up with Carol Applegate was that it wasn't fair. Why should she get all the hunks? At least she hadn't gotten around to this one yet. "You don't look like any secretary I ever met," she said, touching his hand. "But you do have strong fingers. I'll bet you can type up a storm."

"That's not precisely what I do for Mr. Palance," he informed her haughtily. "Most of my time is spent at a computer terminal, not a typewriter."

"Oh. I didn't mean . . ."

"Quite all right. I am in fact a proficient typist."

"Yeah?" someone asked in a gruff voice. "I suppose that's okay. But how are you at pool?"

Stevens swiveled around on his bar stool to find that the old geezer was standing behind him. "I know my way around a billiard table. Who might you be, sir?"

"Jack. Jack Bensen. Up to a game of eight ball, Mr. Stevens? Or are you going to spend the rest of the night looking down Maureen's blouse?"

"Jack!" Maureen cried. "Hold your tongue! Can't you see the gentleman and I are having a conversation?"

"If he works for Palance, he ain't no gentleman," Jack commented derisively. "And I bet he can't play pool worth a shit, either."

"You, sir, are becoming a nuisance," Stevens said, getting to his feet—a bit unsteadily, he noticed. The ale was indeed potent, seeming to have gone right to his feet. And his mouth. "Mr. Palance is a fine man. I can understand your point of view; to you it must seem as if he's stolen a local girl away from her beau. But that is no reason to pick a fight with me. To be quite honest, I don't approve of their liaison, either."

"You don't?"

"I don't. In the first place it hardly seems . . ."

"Kosher?" Jack offered.

Stevens smiled and stepped closer to Jack.

"Yes! I like that word. It isn't kosher. Besides, it distracts my employer from business."

"Just what is your business in Tithe?"

Straightening his back, Stevens replied quietly, "I'm not at liberty to divulge that information, sir."

"Uh-huh." Jack pondered that for a moment, watching the other man sway slightly as he stood there. Then he smiled. "I guess I owe you an apology, Mr. Stevens."

"Apology accepted, Mr. Bensen."

"Call me Jack. And I'm sorry about saying you couldn't play pool too. I was just trying to rile you up a bit, get you to pay for a game."

"That apology I'll not accept. Instead, I'm going to thrash you good and proper." Stevens turned back to the bar and took out his wallet, putting a sheaf of bills in front of Maureen. "Those machines take twenty-five-cent pieces, do they not?" She nodded. "Then I'll have a handful. And another pint. The rest is yours, my dear."

Her eyes widened. "Thanks! Quarters and another ale, coming right up."

He took them and headed for the pool tables. Jack lingered at the bar. "Bring me some more ice water when you get a chance, Maureen. If you're not too mad about me stealing away your new boyfriend?"

Maureen studied the slender, fastidiously dressed Stevens and chuckled. "It could be interesting. Anyway, I have the feeling he'll be here until closing time."

"Count on it," Jack told her, grinning broadly. "I imagine he'll be wanting another ale in a few minutes. He's so tense. And we both want him nice and relaxed, don't we?"

15

The sidewalks were buried, so Sean had to walk in the street. In a little while the road crews wouldn't bother clearing that, either. All the shops were closing. In fact, he was one of the few people out. It was Christmas Eve, time for everyone to go home, sit in front of a roaring fire, and drink eggnog, which is exactly what he intended to do once he closed the pub and got to Carol's house.

Of course, that wasn't the only thing he wanted to do when he got there. That would depend on her, the whereabouts of Richard Palance, and a couple of other imponderables. It was still early and worth a try. But he didn't hold out much hope for it being as easy to get close to her now as it had been at the pub earlier.

He patted the coat pocket containing Carol's present. Actually, it was and it wasn't. They'd made a pact to give food or drink for Christmas. This gift would come later—if all went well tonight, of course. If not . . .

Sean refused to think about that possibility. Instead he started singing at the top of his lungs, caroling the whole length of town to the doorstep of his own pub.

"Merry Christmas!" he bellowed as he came through the door. The small crowd bellowed it right back at him. He took off his coat and went to the bar, where Maureen was polishing glasses. "I think it's nearly time we threw these good folks out on their ears, Maureen."

She indicated the pool tables with a motion of her head. "Jack might take objection to that, at least for another hour or so."

"What's going on?" Sean asked, moving to the end of the bar to pour himself a cup of hot coffee. "He find a sucker?"

"More like a worthy opponent."

Sean took a seat, leaning back against the bar to watch them play for a few minutes. Although Jack was holding his own, he was working at it harder than usual for him; the other man was an excellent player with a very educated defensive style.

"I see what you mean," he said. "They've got themselves a tournament going there. Who is that guy?"

"Mr. Stevens. Richard Palance's personal secretary."

"Is it now?" Sean grinned. Somehow, he didn't think pool was the only game Jack was playing over there. "Jack okay for money?"

Maureen nodded. "Stevens is paying for all the games, win or lose. Nice of him, don't you think?"

"Did I detect a certain twinkle in your eye

when you said that? Or is he just a good tipper?"

"Both," she replied. "He does have a roll in his pocket that'd choke Jack's mule. But I also happen to think he's pretty cute. Not as cute as you . . ."

"Maureen."

"I know." She sighed. "Off limits. Anyway, he's from out of town and I don't have any family to spend Christmas with, so I wouldn't mind sticking around until they finish playing. If you get my drift."

Sean reached into his pocket and brought out the keys to the pub. "Say no more," he said, pushing them across the bar to her. "As it so happens, I was sort of counting on you to do the honors tonight anyway."

"Oh? Have plans of your own this evening?"

"A few."

He smiled and got to his feet, then made the rounds of his customers, making sure they were having a good time. When Jack and Stevens finished the game they were on, he went over to see how they were doing as well.

"How's it going, Jack?" Sean asked.

"What do you see me doing?"

"Racking the balls for your victorious opponent."

"Then don't ask silly questions. Have you met Mr. Percival Stevens there?" Jack raised his eyebrows. "He's Palance's personal secretary."

"Haven't had the pleasure." He shook hands

with the other man. "Sean O'Phaelan. How do you find my pub, Mr. Stevens?"

Stevens blinked at him owlishly. "Why, one simply comes right down the hill and there it is, isn't it?" He laughed gaily. "Sorry, couldn't resist. It's a lovely place. Delightful ambiance."

"Percy has an unusual sense of humor," Jack said.

"Uh, yeah." Sean studied him. Percy was also well on his way to getting plastered. "I can see you two are doing just fine."

"Right as rain," Stevens assured him. "A good friend to share a game and a tale, a good pint of ale, and a truly smashing barmaid." He leaned closer to Sean and added in a conspiratorial tone, "I trust I'm not repeating my employer's gaffe in that regard."

"Pardon?"

"Miss Maureen. She's not . . . taken? So to speak?"

Sean chuckled. "No, Percy. Miss Maureen is quite free. So to speak. Nice of you to ask first."

"Yes. Well, all gentleman are created equal, but some are more gentlemanly than others," he said quietly. Then he put two fingers to his lips. "Goodness! I am telling tales out of school tonight! If you'll excuse me."

The slender, well-dressed man tottered off toward the restroom. Sean put a hand on Jack's shoulder. "Okay, Jack. He's good, but by my reckoning he's also got about three quarts worth of my best ale in him. You're not sharking poor old Percy, are you?"

"Me?" Jack slapped his leg and laughed. "Seriously, I don't think I could. He may be a gentleman, but some part of his youth was misspent. Handles his cue like a surgeon would a scalpel, and if anything he's getting better as he goes along. The only thing that ale has done to him so far is loosen up his legs. And his lips."

"I noticed. Say anything interesting?"

"A couple of things," Jack replied. "Do you want the good news or the bad news first?"

Sean frowned. "The bad I guess."

"Palance has plans to spend Christmas Eve with Carol."

"Shit. But I expected as much. Any idea when he might show up at her house?"

"That's the good news. You were right about him going to Denver today. And he's not back yet. Stevens thinks the Highway Patrol probably turned him around."

"Could be," Sean said.

"He also told me the phones are out up at the condo complex, maybe the whole town for all I know."

"Gee, that's a shame."

Jack poked him in the ribs. "So what are you standing around here for? It looks like you've got a clear track to me. Full speed ahead!"

"I'm still not going to railroad her, Jack. But it is time I got moving. By the way, if it gets too late and the weather too bad, you're welcome to use my apartment for the night. Maureen has the keys."

"Thanks, Sean."

He stopped by the bar on his way out. "Shut her down at ten, Maureen. And please cut your new friend off before he gets too toasted. I don't want him barfing on the tables."

"No problem there, boss," she assured him with a wicked grin. "I want him in perfect working order too, you know."

16

Carol had taken some antacid, showered, then dressed in a white turtleneck topped with her favorite fuzzy red sweater and what she considered her good jeans—meaning they were still dark blue. Now she was sitting in the living room, nibbling on odds and ends from her refrigerator and watching a classic Christmas movie on television.

She always cried when Scrooge awoke a changed man. This year it really opened the floodgates for some reason. So when she heard a noise on her front porch, it took a minute and a handful of tissues before she could even answer the door.

"I'm sorry, Richard, I . . . Sean!"

"Carol!"

He was standing there, a pair of snowshoes in one hand and a great big stoneware jug in the other, beaming at her as if he hadn't even heard her mention the name of his rival.

"What are you doing here?" she asked.

"Bringing you your Christmas present, of course," Sean replied. He propped his snowshoes up against the outside wall and held up the jug. It made ominous gurgling noises. "Grandma's killer eggnog. Old family recipe."

Carol looked at him suspiciously. "I thought we'd agreed you were going to give me some time to think."

"No, you said it and dashed out the door. I didn't agree to anything. Are you going to ask me in, or wait until your living room is full of snow?"

The wind was blowing much harder now, whipping snow in every direction. She shivered. "Oh . . . all right. But only for a minute."

"Thanks." He came in, immediately taking off his coat and heavy canvas overshoes so the snow adhering to them wouldn't soak her carpet. "I swear two inches fell in the fifteen minutes it took me to get here from the pub," Sean told her. "It's going to be a weird night and no mistake."

Carol didn't argue. What with the phone call from her mother, her overly emotional reaction to the movie, and now Sean's unexpected arrival, she was already having a strange Christmas Eve. And what on earth had happened to Richard?

"Are the roads bad?"

"Roads? What roads? What you have on this end of town are snowdrifts with asphalt underneath. *Way* underneath," he said, tapping his leg at midthigh. "The only people crazy enough to drive on them—or rather drive through them—are the four-wheelers. It looked like a blast, but I decided I'd rather snowshoe and make sure I arrived."

"Lucky me."

Sean studied her face. "Have you been crying?"

"A movie on television just got to me, that's all," she told him, dabbing at the corner of her eyes. "Silly."

"Well, no more of that on Christmas Eve!" He shook the jug. "Time to forget our troubles and toast the season!"

What the hell. Killer eggnog sounded about right for the way she was feeling this evening. "Okay. Come on into the kitchen and I'll get us some cups."

Carol led the way and he followed, admiring the gentle sway of her rear end. He'd told Jack he hadn't planned on railroading her. While that was true, he hadn't forgotten how readily she had come back into his arms that afternoon, either. His grandmother had always quoted a favorite adage when things got confusing: Where there's a will, there's a way. After two weeks, Sean had one hell of a hard will.

And her recipe for eggnog.

He poured some into the red glass cups she got from her cupboard, then gave her one and took one for himself, raising it in a toast. "To love!" he exclaimed.

Carol glared at him. "Sean O'Phaelan!"

"How kind! But you can't drink a toast to me yet. It's not your turn." Sean touched his cup to hers. "Love!"

"Bah!" She took a big swallow. "Hum . . . humm . . . hummm!" Carol felt as if the top of head were coming off. Her eyes went wide and her mouth dropped open, her voice nothing more than a hoarse whisper. "Eggnog my eye! What the hell is this stuff?"

"More nog than egg," Sean admitted. He sipped at his own, grinned, then finished it off. "Tasty. Not quite as much kick as Grandma's, but mighty tasty."

"Any more kick and you'd be picking me up off the floor." Once the initial burn wore off, however, Carol decided she agreed with him. It was a spicy taste, nutmeg and cinnamon, with just a hint of clove. She took another sip. "But it does kind of grow on you, doesn't it?"

Sean nodded. "Refill?"

"Well . . . I guess so. It is Christmas."

He gave them each another splash and recorked the big earthenware jug. "I'll just set the rest out on the back porch. If you don't keep it real cold, it has a tendency toward spontaneous combustion."

"I'll bet." Carol leaned against the counter. A blast of frigid air hit her when Sean opened the back door, but this time it felt good. "Is my face red?"

"Only a healthy Christmas glow," Sean replied. "Looks very nice on you, too. Mind if I sit by the fire for a while and thaw out my toes?"

She knew exactly what he was trying to thaw out. Her. To a certain extent he was succeeding. It wasn't just the potent eggnog, either. Being near Sean always made things stir inside her, and tonight that was especially true. With Richard on the way, though, she decided she could trust herself around him for a little while.

"All right. But I'm expecting company, Sean," Carol informed him. "So no funny stuff."

Sean turned and headed back to the living room, hiding his smile. "Speaking of funny, Stevens dropped by the pub this evening. He and Jack were still playing pool when I left and having a ball. They make quite a pair."

"Stevens? Richard's secretary?" She frowned. "I only met him once, but he struck me as rather stuffy, definitely not the party type. Did you talk to him?"

"Just to say hello. He had other things on his mind, like ale, beating Jack, and ogling Maureen."

Sean sat down on her couch near the fireplace. Carol was so surprised by what he was telling her that she sat down beside him without thinking, as she had on many other cold winter nights.

"Really?" Her eyebrows shot up. "How strange!"

"Not at all. My bitter ale has been known to unstuff a few stuffed shirts. Besides, when the cat's away . . ."

"The cat?"

"Didn't you know? Richard went to Denver this morning."

Carol looked at him. The smile on his face

was smugly self-satisfied. "What are you trying to tell me, Sean?"

He draped his arm on the couch behind her back. "That Porsche of his is a fine automobile, great in the snow up to a point. I imagine Richard passed that point quite some time ago. If he's the company you're expecting, you could have a long wait."

"He would have called me."

"I hear we're having trouble with the phones."

"My mother got through earlier," Carol objected. "And she's in Hawaii." All of a sudden she felt quite vulnerable. She crossed her arms over her breasts.

Sean settled his arm comfortably around her shoulders. "That's west. The storm is coming in from the east."

"Still . . ." She trailed off, remembering the strange way the phone had rung just before her mother called. "I'd better call the Highway Patrol! He may be stranded!"

She started to get up, but he wrapped his arm around her waist and pulled her back down beside him. "I doubt that. They probably didn't even let him up the pass. But since I wouldn't put it past him to buy a ride up with somebody else, he may show his face yet."

"But I—"

"Tell you what," Sean interrupted, pulling her hip tightly against his. "I'll keep you company until he does. Even if it takes all night."

Carol struggled for a moment. It wasn't any use. "I really do have to have more time, Sean."

"What's wrong? We're still friends, aren't we? Can't one friend comfort another in her hour of need?"

She wished he hadn't used that particular word. Need was exactly what she felt. The wind was howling, Grandma's killer eggnog was coursing through her veins, and there was Sean, holding her tight in front of a cozy fire on what she had always considered the most magical night of the year.

"That depends on what sort of comfort the friend has in mind," Carol replied. She looked down at her lap. "For instance, do you really think unbuttoning my jeans is going to make me forget that Richard may be stuck somewhere?"

Sean chuckled. "I'd stake The Naked Waitress on it."

"Then hand over the keys, because . . . Oh!"

"Aren't you the festive one? Red sweater, white turtleneck, green panties." He hummed softly as he rubbed her stomach. "Mmm! My little candy cane!"

"Stop that!" she exclaimed, doing her best to keep him from pulling her turtleneck out of the waist of her jeans. "What are you trying to do?"

"Cool you down." Sean looked at her face. "Still flushed with worry," he announced. Then he slipped his hand under her turtleneck, gently cupping her breasts. "You're burning up!

I could get a cold compress, but time is of the essence. Maybe I can absorb some of that heat this way."

He lay down on the couch, pulling her on top of him, his tongue plunging deeply into her mouth. Moaning, Carol tried to pull away, but found her arms too weak and her strength of will rapidly evaporating. At last she gave in, settling herself atop him and responding to his impassioned kiss in kind. Sean's hands wandered down her back to the waist of her unbuttoned jeans, then beneath the elastic of her festive panties, holding her buttocks as he pressed himself against her.

"There," he whispered in her ear. "I'll bet you're not worried about him now."

"Who?"

She kissed his throat, her tongue darting out to taste him. Like her, he had on a turtleneck, covered by a thick wool shirt. It scratched her bare stomach and frustrated her desire to feel his skin against hers.

To hell with caution, problematic relationships, and fear. And to hell with Richard. Carol wanted Sean and she wanted him right now. She pulled away from him, struggling out of her sweater. Sean sat up and removed his shirt, then at her urging his turtleneck as well. His chest looked a great deal like that gladiator she had sculpted, broad and well muscled. The firelight reflected in his eyes made them gleam; she knew hers were gleaming as well, at the thought of what else he and the statue had in common.

But another thought intruded upon her excitement as she looked into his eyes. As much as she wanted him, Carol knew a night of passion wasn't going to change the facts. Sean probably thought it would, and it just might for a few days or even weeks. Sooner or later, however, the pressure of making a commitment would return. And she would back away from it, hurting him all over again.

It wasn't right to lead him on, allow her desires and weak willpower to make him think everything was going to be all right. She had to tell him.

"Sean . . ."

He groaned. "Oh, no! Not now!"

"Yes. Right now. I have to tell you something."

When he turned away from her and glared at the front door, Carol realized he wasn't even listening. At least not to her. Something was coming up her driveway, or rather trying to; she could now hear the roar of a powerful engine being worked to within an inch of its endurance as whatever vehicle it propelled slipped, lurched, and hopped its way toward her house.

Finally the beams of its headlights flashed across the closed curtains of her front window. The straining engine balked, gave an explosive backfire, then stopped. They heard a door slam, then the sound of someone grunting and cursing as he struggled through the deep snow up to her porch. If a knock could sound apologetic, this one did. But after all, Carol thought, a punctual man like Richard would be sorry for arriving late.

17

"Dammit!" Sean muttered. "Not now!"

Part of Carol wanted to yell the same thing at the top of her lungs. Not now, just when she'd worked up the courage to finish this once and for all. But another part of her was calling her a liar, because what she felt most of all was relief.

Coward.

Absolutely. Carol got off the couch, grabbed her sweater and pulled it on, then stuffed her turtleneck back into her pants and buttoned them up. On her way to the door, she cast a sidelong glance at Sean. He stood up, put his hands on his hips, and faced the door with a belligerent expression.

"Well?" she prompted.

"Well what?"

"Put your shirt on for heaven's sake!"

Sean shrugged his broad, bare shoulders. "Why?"

"Go ahead then! Make a fool of yourself and see if I care!" So what if it was obvious what had been going on? Richard would be mad, Sean was already boiling, so maybe they'd fight with each other and leave her alone for a while. Still, as she opened the door, she said, "This isn't what it looks like, Richard. Sean—"

"Merry Christmas!"

Carol looked at the man standing in her doorway and just about fainted. But she quickly regained her wits. "Shove it up your nose, Frank! Goddammit! I thought I told you I never wanted to see your face around here again!"

"But it's Christmas!"

"Get the hell out of here!" Carol yelled. She tried to close the door, but her ex-husband wedged his rotund body between it and the door jamb. "Get off my property and out of my life!"

"You must be joking," Frank said. He had some trouble getting the words out, mainly because Carol was banging the door against his chest. "I . . . oof! I barely made it onto your property in the first place. It'll take a . . . ouch! A snowplow to get my truck out of the drift it's stuck in."

"Then walk!" She hit him with the door again. It probably wasn't hurting him, what with the heavy coat he had on, but it was certainly making her feel better. "Crawl if you have to. I don't care. Just go!"

Frank was managing to slip inside in spite of her abuse. "Where? The pass is closed and there's a blizzard coming on, Carol. Hell, the wind-chill factor is already low enough to kill me before I could get a mile. Where do you suggest I go?"

"Straight to hell!"

"Carol, stop it," Sean said. He put a hand on her shoulder and pulled her away from the door. "Let him in."

With the sudden release of the door, Frank literally fell in, landing on the living-room carpet with a thud. He looked up at the big, bare-chested man towering over him and smiled weakly. "Gee, thanks! I was dying out there!"

"You might die in here if you don't explain yourself," Sean told him. He shut the front door, scowling. "So I suggest you start talking, and it had better be good."

Carol was scowling down at him too. Feeling at a disadvantage, he got slowly to his feet. Frank was a fairly large man himself, but Sean still had about five inches and at least fifty pounds on him. And unlike Sean, his bulk was no longer in the form of muscle.

In the years since Carol had divorced him, he'd totally given in to his tendency to put on weight around his middle. He was still rather handsome, with his blue eyes, sandy blond hair, and full beard, but at the moment both hair and beard were sodden with melting snow, making him look scruffy and unkempt.

"Well," Frank began hesitantly, "it's like this. I always come see Carol at Christmastime and—"

"And I told you never to do it again!" Carol said. "I don't want to hear this. Where's my ax?"

Sean kept his hand on her shoulder. "Calm down."

"I was going to stay away this year, Carol,"

Frank assured her quickly. "Really. But something just kept calling me back. I was in Grand Junction, trying to put together a deal with some Australian businessmen who've developed this new gold extraction process. I've got an option on a site piled high with old tailings, see, and I figure if . . ." He trailed off, seeing the anger growing in Sean's eyes. "Anyway, there I was, and something just called to me. Like a voice in my head, you know? Telling me to come and see you."

"Sure," Carol said bitterly. "And I suppose this voice also told you that as long as you were at it, you should try to con me out of the money to close this once-in-a-lifetime deal. Is that about right?"

"Well . . ."

"Get on with it!" Sean exclaimed.

Frank glanced at him nervously. "Before I knew it I was in my truck and headed for Tithe," he blurted. "Once I got here I remembered what happened last time and was going to turn back. Honest I was. But the weather took a turn and they closed the pass. So now I'm stuck. I don't have anywhere else to go, Carol."

He looked and sounded pathetic. His story was certainly the most pathetic of all the tall tales he'd ever told her. But as she stood there, glaring at him and wishing Sean would let her go so she could punch Frank in the nose, she could hear the sound of the wind outside. It rattled her windows and beat on her roof, moaning like a lost soul through the pine trees lining her driveway.

Turning him out on a night like this would be more than cruel; it could quite possibly be construed as murder. And though that thought had crossed her mind on occasion, Carol knew she would never carry it out.

She looked at Sean, then back at Frank, who was standing there dripping on her living-room carpet. "Shit!" she exclaimed, throwing her hands up in a gesture of total submission to fate. "Why not? This is the most screwed up Christmas Eve of my life. Why not complete it by letting my ex-husband spend the night?"

"Thanks, Carol. You won't regret it." Frank pulled off his coat, spraying cold droplets of melted snow all over the place. "As soon as this deal goes through I'll—"

"Shut up, Frank," she said with an exasperated sigh. "Stay right there until I get you a towel."

Carol left the room, shaking her head. Sean grabbed his turtleneck from the back of the couch and pulled it on. He was still scowling at Frank. "Your timing sucks, pal."

"Sorry. But I had to get out of that storm. Barely made it here as it was, and I've got chains on all four wheels." He extended his hand. "No hard feelings?"

"Stop dripping on my couch!" Carol yelled as she came back into the living room.

Sean shook hands with the other man. "Sean O'Phaelan."

"Oh. Right. Frank Case."

Carol hit him in the face with a towel. "There. Dry off. And take those damn boots off too."

When he'd done as she asked, Frank went to warm himself by the fire. With his red flannel shirt and the weight he'd put on, he looked like Santa Claus getting ready to pop back up the chimney. His booze-reddened nose completed the effect.

"I don't suppose I could get a drop of Christmas cheer, by any chance?" he asked.

Sean grinned. "I've just the thing. There's eggnog on the back porch." He grabbed his glass. "I'll pour."

Frank didn't have to be asked twice. As Sean went past her, Carol grabbed his arm. "Just because I'm letting him stay, that doesn't mean we have to be nice to him."

"Carol Applegate! Where's your Christmas spirit?"

"It blew out the door when he came in," she replied sourly. "After all I've told you about Frank, how can you be so friendly?"

"I'm just pouring the man a drink. In fact, I think I'll pour him several." Sean winked and added in a low voice, "Maybe he'll pass out and we can get back to what we were doing."

"Fat chance on both counts."

"You know me. Ever the optimist."

He patted her lovingly on the derriere and went to join Frank in the kitchen. Carol sat down on the couch and put her face in her hands. "Why me?" she muttered.

The back door opened and closed, letting more cold air into the house. She stood up and added a few logs to the fire. At least there were two strong men around to split firewood should the need arise.

"Hoohah!" Frank yelled at the top of his lungs. "Damn! That'll put lead in your pencil!"

"Yes indeedy! More?" Sean asked.

"Well, you have to believe in something. I believe I'll have another snort. How about you?"

"Don't mind if I do."

Carol groaned. This was just peachy. The man she didn't want to love and the man she loved to hate, together under the same roof, getting zonked in her kitchen. She had half a mind to go join them. It might be the only way she'd get through this without losing her mind.

They came back into the living room, grinning from ear to ear. Sean was carrying the jug. "How about a toast, Carol? It's your turn to do the honors, I believe."

She frowned at him for a moment, then held out her cup with a resigned sigh. Sean filled it. "To forbearance," she said, touching each of their cups in turn. "May mine last through this storm."

"Here, here." Sean gazed at her pointedly, arching his eyebrows. "Mine too."

"Strange toast," Frank said, but he drank to it

anyway. Then he raised his cup again. "I've got one. To missing comrades!"

"What's that supposed to mean?"

He shrugged. "I don't know. I just always liked it."

They finished the eggnog in their cups. But as Sean was about to pour another round, he stopped and again glowered at the front door. "What was that?"

"A clatter?" Frank suggested.

Carol dashed to the living-room window and threw open the curtains. "Now what's the matter?" she wondered aloud.

Sean joined her. "Who's here?"

"Well, it sure as hell ain't Santa and his eight tiny reindeer," Frank said. "Unless he's taken to driving a snowplow."

The huge machine rumbled to a stop in front of her house. Out of necessity it had cleared a path for itself up the driveway, but that wasn't going to do Carol much good, because the wall of glistening powder it pushed to one side buried both Frank's truck and her van.

Not that anyone was going to be leaving for a while in any case. The snow wasn't really falling anymore, it was blowing across the valley in a near vertical plane of white. From their vantage point, it was like looking through a constantly shifting sheet of gauze, so thick that they could barely make out the bundled-up figure that jumped out of the plow, waved to the driver, then started wallowing through the hip-deep snow toward her porch.

There was a gaily wrapped present in his arms, but the look on his face wasn't jolly when he saw Carol standing at the window with two men. He banged on the front door.

Carol opened it. Richard stepped inside and she closed it again immediately, feeling the bite of wind-driven snow on her cheeks. The bottom half of him was completely white, and from the waist up his cashmere coat was peppered with ice crystals. His teeth were chattering.

He glared at Sean, who glared right back. Frank just looked confused. Richard focused his glare on Carol and managed to say "W-what is the m-meaning of this, C-Carol?"

"Beats the hell out of me," she replied. "But whatever it is, we're all stuck with it for the rest of the night. So you might as well join the party, Richard." Carol motioned for Sean to fill her cup with eggnog, which she then handed to the shivering Richard. "Here. Drink that. Then I'll see if I can't find you something warm and dry to put on."

Richard sniffed it. "W-what—"

"Just drink it. It'll heat you right up."

That sounded fine to Richard. He gulped it gratefully. Then he gasped and leaned back against the door, his dark eyes open wide. Color rushed to his face and his teeth stopped chattering. After a moment, he held the cup out.

"More, please."

Sean filled it for him. "I guess I was wrong about you, Palance," he said.

"How so, O'Phaelan?"

"You're a money-grubbing, woman-stealing son of a bitch, but at least you're not a wimp."

His eyes narrowed. "I beg your pardon!"

"You damn well should, asshole."

"No one says that to Richard Palance and—"

"Richard Palance!" Frank cried. "I thought you looked familiar, you bastard! You're the corporate raider who screwed up my bid for that Alaskan property last year! When that deal fell through I ended up working in a stinking cannery for nine months to pay my partners back so they wouldn't break my legs!"

He lunged at Richard. Sean held him back. "Calm down, Frank. If anybody's going to bust him one, it'll be me!"

"If either of you touches me I'll have you in jail on assault charges so fast your heads will spin!" Richard told them. "Macho mountain buffoons!"

"Prissy three-piece bird dog!"

"Conniving shit-heeled weasel!"

Carol just shrugged and started up the stairs, to see if she could find something for Richard to wear. By the way the three of them were arguing, though, she probably shouldn't bother. All that hot air would dry him out in no time.

A confused woman, two aggressively dominant suitors, and her childish ex-husband, all snowed in together on Christmas Eve. "Well," Carol muttered. "So much for a silent night."

18

Richard wasn't at all happy with his attire. The terry-cloth robe Carol had found for him must have been voluminous on her, because it fit him fairly well. But shocking pink was hardly his color. Combined with the floppy green socks she'd given him for his feet, he was painfully aware that he looked ridiculous. Still, he supposed he should be thankful it was warm, dry, and long enough to cover his bare legs.

"I put your things in the dryer, Richard," Carol told him as he emerged from the downstairs bathroom. "So you won't have to wear that—" She clapped one hand over her mouth, doing her best not to laugh. "Oh, Richard! I'm sorry, but you look so funny!"

Frank didn't bother hiding his amusement. He was laughing so hard he practically fell off the couch. "I love it! Hey, baby! Come on over here and we'll pitch some woo!"

Showing great aplomb under the circumstances, Richard walked into the room and took a seat by the fire, his head held high. Sean was at the fireplace, using a poker to settle the logs he'd just added to the flames. He glanced at

Richard, grinned, then turned back to his project.

"Well?" Richard asked. "Aren't you going to have some fun at my expense, O'Phaelan?"

"Nah. Too easy."

Richard crossed his legs, rearranging the robe to cover them. "Go ahead. I can hardly wait to hear the sort of infantile remark a man like you will come up with."

Sean stood up. "A man like me? You don't have any idea what sort of man I am, Palance. You, on the other hand, are an open book."

"Oh?"

"You're a user, a deceiver. And not just Carol, either. Guys like you always rise to the top because you don't care who you step on to get there. It doesn't matter what you wear; a jerk in a five-hundred-dollar suit is still a jerk."

"God save us from liberals," Richard said with a cool smile. "It amazes me you've done as well in business as you have, O'Phaelan. Then again, I don't suppose one can actually refer to a little mountain pub as much of a business compared to the investment empire I've forged."

"At least it's mine," Sean returned. "Created by the sweat of my own brow. And where do you get off criticizing private enterprise? We're the ones who work and slave to make something out of nothing, then some 'investor' comes along, usually as a prelude to a take-over. You're just another shark, circling around waiting for someone to start sinking so you can join the corporate feeding frenzy."

"I can only agree with one facet of your analogy. In business as in nature, the law of the jungle prevails. Survival of the fittest, you know."

Frank gave him a raspberry. "Bull! Survival of the fattest is more like it. You gorge, we starve."

"At least O'Phaelan has some concept of what's going on," Richard said. "While you, Case, are a complete moron."

"I don't have to sit here and be insulted by a guy who looks like a cross-dressing elf," Frank said, getting to his feet. "Where's that jug?"

"In the kitchen," Sean replied. "I'll come with you. There's something about the air in here I don't like." He looked pointedly at Richard. "Must be the smell of the jungle clinging to him."

"Good one, pal!"

"We are not pals, Frank," Sean told him, "I'd prefer the company of a sewer rat to yours. The minute this storm blows over you're history."

Carol had had enough. "Stop picking on each other! Storm or no storm, you're all three going to be out on your butts if you don't shut up! You're driving me crazy!" She stomped off toward the back of the house to check the clothes dryer, still yelling. "It's Christmas Eve, dammit! Either get along or get out!"

"I do believe she means that," Richard said.

Sean nodded. "Count on it."

"And Carol can get real nasty when she's pissed," Frank agreed. "I guess we'd better make peace." He glared at Richard. "Or at least pretend to."

They looked at each other for a moment, sharing the same sullen expression. Then Sean snapped his fingers. "I know. Why don't we shift the field of combat? A game of cards, maybe?"

Frank scratched his bearded chin. "Yeah. That'd make it seem like we were getting along, wouldn't it?"

"Whist?" Richard suggested.

Sean said, "I was thinking more along the lines of poker."

"Great!" Frank started to slap Sean on the back to show his approval but thought better of it. "Maybe I can win some money off of this . . . this gentleman."

"I'll clean you both out," Sean vowed.

Richard cleared his throat and spoke in a patronizing tone. "I'm no stranger to the game, gentlemen. Apparently neither are you. As I undoubtedly have enough money in my wallet to buy every pot, I suggest we play table stakes."

"Good idea," Frank said, checking his own wallet. "How about a hundred bucks?"

"We may as well play for pennies," Richard commented disdainfully. "But if that's all you have, I'll take it."

"Like hell you will!"

"Ssh!" Sean put his finger to his lips. "I've just had a thought. Carol won't like us trying to break each other any more than she likes us bickering. Maybe you're right, Palance."

"About whist?"

Sean made a face. "No. We should play for pennies. That'll make Carol happy. And after all, a winner is a winner no matter what the stakes, right?"

"Fine with me," Richard said.

"Me too." Frank went to the rolltop desk in the hallway. "She used to keep a deck of cards in this thing at our old house. Let's see . . ."

"I'll go clear off the kitchen table and raid the jar of pennies in Carol's pantry," Sean announced. He chuckled. "And pour us a round of eggnog, of course. To keep us warm."

Richard stood up. "Speaking of which, I'm going to see if my clothes are dry. How do women wear dresses? There's a terrible draft up this robe!"

"Maybe if you put on some pantyhose," Sean told him.

"Yeah!" Frank chortled. "That'd really complete the look, Palance."

"Penny ante or not, I'm going to enjoy raking you two over the coals," Richard grumbled.

Carol was just pulling his pants out of the dryer when Richard stepped into the utility room at the end of the downstairs hallway. His suit coat was already on a hanger nearby. Both would need the attention of a professional dry cleaner after this abuse, but wrinkles were the last things on Richard's mind at the moment.

He came up behind her in his stocking feet

and put his arms around her waist. "In all the fuss, I forgot to wish you a Merry Christmas. Did you see the present I placed under your tree?"

"Yes, thank you," Carol replied. "Yours is in the refrigerator. Just some cookies."

"If you made them, I'm sure they'll be manna from heaven." He nibbled on her neck. "It's a shame we can't be alone this evening. Perhaps tomorrow we can—"

"Oh! Stop that!"

It wasn't the nibbling so much as the way he was pressing himself against her buttocks. Carol could feel another present Richard obviously wanted to give her stirring beneath his robe. She squirmed out of his grasp and handed him his pants.

"You'd better put these on. I've had enough surprises pop out at me this evening, thank you."

Richard wasn't going to be deterred that easily. "Don't shy away from me, Carol. I could have died getting to you tonight, you know." He threw his pants over his coat and advanced upon her, until she was backed up against the warm dryer. "The Highway Patrol stopped me just out of Denver, but I lied about my destination and managed to get through. That's how badly I needed to be with you."

"Richard, please . . ."

Leaning forward, he put one hand on either side of her hips, trapping her in place. "My car spun into a snowdrift, but did I stop? No! I got out and started walking. Poor, lovesick fool! If that plow hadn't come along, I surely would have frozen."

Lovesick? More like sex starved! His dark eyes were glittering with a desire so strong it worried her. She'd wanted to know what it was like to be with a man who only had pure, unbridled lust on his mind. If Sean and Frank weren't just down the hall, Carol had the feeling she would be finding out, right there on the utility-room floor.

"I appreciate the sentiment, Richard," she told him, "and all you've been through, but I am not in the mood for this tonight. This isn't the place or time."

"No, but soon! I want you, Carol! Feel my need!"

As he thrust his hips forward, she pushed his left arm away and stepped aside. Instead of her soft body, Richard's groin connected solidly with the hard corner of the dryer.

"Oof!" Richard grabbed himself and bent over, groaning.

Carol heard footsteps. No sense letting this escalate into a brawl. She patted Richard on the head and left the utility room, meeting Sean in the hallway.

"What the hell's taking so long?" Sean asked.

"Richard was just telling me how awful his trip up was. I gather it was a painful experience. But he's got a grip on himself now," she explained with a smile. "It's been awfully quiet out here. What are you up to?"

"We thought we'd take your advice and channel our energy in another direction. Just a friendly poker game to pass the time."

Carol frowned. "You're not playing for money, are you? I'm not going to have the losers starting a fight."

"Just pennies. Richard wanted to play the high roller, but I told him you wouldn't like it. Care to sit in? They're your pennies, after all."

"Sounds like fun. Hurry up, Richard! The poker game is about to start!"

19

"Your eyes are like emeralds; your skin, alabaster. Your every movement is a song; the touch of your gentle hand a symphony. I worship the delicate curve of your ankles, the womanly fullness of your hips. And your bosom . . ." He trailed off in a sigh. "Well, your bosom is simply beyond words, my lovely Maureen."

"Oh, Percy! You say the sweetest things!"

They were sitting at the bar together, hip to hip, talking quietly though they were all alone in the pub. The last customer had left over an hour ago. From the sound of the wind screaming outside, they should have been long gone by now too.

Jack burst through the back door, accompanied by a small avalanche of snow that had piled up against the rear of The Naked Waitress. He had to lean against the door with all his might to close it on the wicked wind.

"Damn! Good thing I've built a tunnel or two in my day," he said, using his hat to dust snow off his clothes. "Because that's about what I had to do to reach the shed."

"Is your mule all right, Jack?"

"Snug as a bug, Percy. I gave her some food, put her blanket on, and packed hay all around her. Betsy'll be nice and toasty."

He shrugged out of his coat and hung it on a chair, then made a beeline for the pub's enormous pot-bellied stove, an antique that had once been used to heat the entire building. The place had a furnace now, but on a night like this every bit of extra warmth was appreciated.

"I tell you, folks," Jack continued as he warmed his hands, "this is the worst I've seen it in years. Eight- and ten-foot drifts. Wind that'll take your face right off."

"No chance of making it home, then?" Maureen asked.

Jack shook his head. "Not for me or Percy. You might make it since you live so close, but I wouldn't try it without full polar gear. Even then it'd be dicey. Hell, I barely found the shed and that's just ten feet out the back door." He sat down on the raised stone hearth that surrounded the stove, letting the heat soak into his back. "Nope. We're stuck for the duration, I'm afraid."

"Damn! And I'd so hoped to show Maureen the whirlpool spa at the condominium." Percy gazed into her eyes. "You would have looked very fetching amid the swirling water."

"I'm sure it'll clear up by tomorrow. We can have a hot-tub Christmas party," Maureen promised. Then she got a wicked gleam in her eyes. She stood up and stretched her arms over her head, sighing. "Hot water does sound good, though. I'm in need of a shower, and Sean just happens to have one upstairs. I know he said you could use the apartment, Jack, but would you mind if I borrowed it for a while?"

"Go ahead and use it yourself," he replied. "I think I'd better grab one of Sean's sleeping bags and stretch out here by the stove tonight anyway. The furnace is having a hard enough time as it is; somebody should keep feeding the flames in case the power goes, so we don't freeze."

"You're a dear, Jack."

Maureen sauntered off toward the stairs. At the first step, she turned and gave Percy a look that made his ears burn. Obviously she had no intention of showering alone.

"Oh, my!" he exclaimed softly. "There is a Santa Claus!"

"What's that, Percy?" Jack asked.

"Hmm?" He was busy watching the hypnotic motion of Maureen's hips as she slowly climbed the stairs. "I've had a lovely evening, Jack. Thanks so much for the rousing competition. But I wonder if you'd mind . . ."

Jack chuckled. "Go on, son! Take care you don't break Sean's bed, though. I hear tell Maureen can get a bit feisty, if you know what I mean."

From the way his face turned red, he evidently knew exactly what Jack meant. "I shall endeavor to use all due caution."

He was off his stool and up the stairs in the wink of an eye. Jack shook his head and laughed. It was amazing what ale and a well-turned ankle could do to a man. When Percy had walked in he was wound tighter than an eight-day watch and his backbone was stiff as a board. Now he was loose as a goose and his stiffness had settled about three inches below his belt buckle.

Jack went to the bar, poured himself that ever-so-rare fourth beer—after leaving seventy-five cents for it, of course—then took his glass over to the stove and sat down in a nearby chair. Grinning, he propped his feet up on the hearth. For a man who had once spent Christmas Eve in a cave atop the Continental Divide, being trapped in a pub with a hot stove and a cold beer was pretty close to heaven.

He was anxious to tell Sean all the interesting things Percival Stevens had let slip through his ale-loosened lips. But even if Jack could make it to Carol's place tonight, he wouldn't. Tomorrow would be soon enough. The boy had plenty to occupy his mind at the moment.

There was an enormous splash upstairs. Maureen giggled.

"Rub-a-dub-dub!" Percy cried.

Jack sat there, smiling and sipping at his beer, not really eavesdropping but enjoying the sounds drifting down the stairs. They reminded him of his own amorous encounters, of which he'd had his fair share in younger days. He hoped Sean and Carol were putting their time alone to as much good use as Percy and Maureen.

He raised his glass in a toast to the storm raging outside. "Ain't love grand!"

20

"Full house."

"Shit!" Frank threw his cards down in disgust. "Now I know what they mean by the luck of the Irish."

"You do seem to be blessed this evening, O'Phaelan," Richard agreed. "What's your secret?"

Sean gave him the evil eye. "If you mean cheating, I think you know more about that than I do."

"And if you mean Carol, I didn't have to cheat."

"Stop it!"

Carol thumped the kitchen table with her fist, making the pennies rattle. Most of those pennies were in front of Sean. It was hard to tell whether that was due to luck, skill, or his constitution. Poker wasn't the only game going on. Although no one had exactly issued a challenge, a spontaneous contest had broken out among them to see who could handle the most Christmas cheer.

Sean kept trying to put his hand on her thigh, but otherwise he was just ducky. Carol had a slight, rather pleasant ringing in her ears. And though Frank had done his best to follow her into the bathroom a moment ago, it was more wishful thinking than inebriation.

Richard was just plain weird. His speech was fine, except that he occasionally lapsed into French so garbled it sounded like pig-Latin. He walked and moved with his usual elegant bearing, even when he'd missed the kitchen doorway and smacked right into the wall. Come to think of it, though, Carol decided it wasn't so weird after all. He was always perfectly self-contained. Apparently his control over himself was so ingrained it continued even after he was blitzed out of his gourd.

As a pub owner who thought he'd seen every reaction to alcohol there was, this delicate balance intrigued Sean no end. And naturally he was doing his best to upset it. He filled everyone's cup from the seemingly bottomless jug, then raised his in a toast.

"To green!" he exclaimed, looking directly at Carol.

Frank puzzled over that for a moment. "Oh, green like a shamrock, eh?" Sean shook his head no. "Green as in greener pastures?"

"Close," he replied, bobbing his eyebrows up and down.

"Money!" Richard guessed.

"And you went out with this man?" Sean asked Carol. "No, Richard, not money, though I imagine you hold that in higher esteem than what I'm thinking of that's covered in green. Hey, that almost rhymes! I'll try again."

Carol was blushing furiously. "Sean! Don't you dare!"

"I'm dreaming of the green a lady might wear," Sean continued blithely, "at Christmas-time, upon her derriere!"

"Oh, yeah!" Frank cried. "That's a tradition! To Carol's green panties!" He downed his egg-nog and belched.

Carol must have been just a bit more tipsy than she realized. Glowering at Sean, she exclaimed, "Okay, smart guy! Let's see what color yours are!" She grabbed him by the belt and unzipped his pants. "Look who's talking! Red!"

"Mine're pink," Frank announced. "Used to be white until I washed 'em with a maroon sweatshirt."

Sean looked at Richard. "Well? We have to be fair, here. What color are yours?"

He was just sitting there, staring off into space. His eggnog was all gone too. At last he blinked, looked at Carol, and asked, "What shade of green?"

"Christmas green, of course," she replied. "Why?"

Richard seemed extremely disappointed. "Dear me. I'm wearing citrus. We clash." Then his eyes closed and he slipped off his chair to the floor.

"Gotcha!" Sean exclaimed triumphantly, patting the jug.

"I thought he'd never leave." Frank crawled

under the table to have a look. "Out cold. Let's pick his pockets!"

"Get away!" Carol told him as she joined him under the table. She patted Richard's cheeks, trying to bring him around. He started to snore. "I think Richard's through for the evening. Somebody help me get him into one of the downstairs bedrooms."

Sean was happy to oblige. "Grab his legs, Frank. I'll get his arms."

With Carol leading the way, they carried Richard out of the kitchen and down the hall to the first bedroom on the right. She used it mainly for storage, so it was hardly the sort of opulent sleeping quarters Richard was used to. He didn't seem to mind. The two men plopped him unceremoniously on the bed.

"I suppose we'll have to undress him," Sean said.

Carol grinned. "I'll do it."

"In a pig's eye! Give me a hand, Frank."

It was a struggle, but they finally got him down to briefs and T-shirt, then stuffed him under the covers, tucking them in so he wouldn't roll out. Carol left the bedside lamp on, though she doubted he'd need it.

"He was right, you know," Sean told her as she closed the door on their way out. "You clash."

She ignored him. "I don't understand it. We've all had about the same amount to drink. I'm lighter than any of you, and all I feel is a nice buzz."

"Can't handle his eggnog, I guess."

Carol thought she detected just a tad too much innocence in Sean's voice. "All right. What'd you do to him?"

"Come on, Carol," Frank objected. "Get off the guy's back. It all came out of the same jug."

He headed for the bathroom. Carol followed Sean into the kitchen. "The same jug," she muttered, picking it up and giving it a shake. She frowned. "There's something strange about this thing. And I just realized that you were always in charge of pouring."

"Be careful with that! It's an heirloom!"

After removing the cork, Carol peered into the neck of the big stoneware container. Then she glared at Sean. "It has a trick spout inside!"

"Okay. You caught me," Sean admitted sheepishly. "My Grandma made a mean batch of eggnog at Christmas, but that was the only time she approved of strong drink. Grandpa had other ideas. He and a like-minded friend of his—who just happened to be a master potter—came up with a way to have a nip without Grandma getting wise. Pour one way, she got a glass of sweet cider. The other way, they got cider laced with grain alcohol. Gives extra zing to eggnog too."

"Sean Patrick O'Phaelan!"

"Funny, that's just the way Grandma yelled at Grandpa the day he got too tipsy and forgot which way to hold the jug," Sean said. He took a step back from her. "Then she bopped him on the nose. You wouldn't do that, would you?"

"Don't bet on it, you skunk!" She clenched her fist.

Frank returned from the bathroom. "Pour me another, Sean! Oops! You two aren't going to fight, are you?"

"Not if I can help it. I have other things in mind," Sean replied. He arched his eyebrows at Carol. "I didn't want 'em both on my hands at the same time. What do you say? One down, one to go?"

"Do what you want! You can both pass out on the floor for all I care! I'm going to bed!"

She turned on her heel and stalked out of the kitchen. Frank wisely elected to stay where he was, but Sean followed, catching her hand as she started up the stairs. "Don't be like this, Carol. Okay, so it wasn't a nice thing to do. I'm sorry. I only wanted to make sure I had you to myself tonight."

"Sure. And just what were you going to do with your trick jug if they hadn't showed up?"

"You don't think I would have—"

"I don't know what to think!" Carol interrupted, yanking her hand out of his grasp. "I told you I was confused and needed time. You didn't let that stop you. How do I know how far you'd go?"

Sean glared at her defiantly. "That's absurd! Be honest with yourself for once, Carol. It wasn't eggnog that made you act the way you did at the pub earlier, or even a few hours ago on the couch. I don't have to get you drunk. All I have to do is touch you."

He reached out to caress her cheek. Carol shied away, knowing he was right. "Don't! Leave me alone, can't you? You, Richard, Frank, all of you! Just leave me alone!"

With that she dashed upstairs and slammed her bedroom door, fuming. She sat on her bed for a while, trying to calm down. Men! It was time for a drastic Christmas change, all right. Celibacy.

Carol could hear them talking in the kitchen, but their voices were too low to make out the words. Then other noises reached her. Water running. Frank gargling in an annoying way she remembered all too well. Footsteps on the stairs. She tensed, knowing it was Sean, but in a moment she heard him brushing his teeth in the upstairs bathroom and relaxed again. He'd obviously decided to do as she demanded of him and leave her alone. For tonight at least.

Sean emerged a few minutes later and crossed the landing to the other upstairs bedroom. The door closed. Finally the house was quiet. She peeked through the keyhole to make sure the coast was clear, quickly went to brush the strange taste of eggnog off her own teeth, then came back to her room and made sure the door was double locked behind her.

In the summer—or with Sean—she slept in the nude. But all she had to keep her warm tonight was her anger, so she donned a pale-yellow flannel nightgown and climbed into bed, pulling the four-poster's heavy curtains closed around her. This was one of those nights she felt like total isolation.

She got it. Not only the house was quiet, *everything* was quiet. Christmas. Three feet of new snow. There was undoubtedly a mouse stirring somewhere, but not much else. Carol lay in the dark, feeling sorry for herself, until at last all that eggnog finally kicked in and she fell asleep.

21

Tick. Tock. It was a pleasant sound. *Tick. Tock.* Hypnotic. *Tick. Tock.* Soothing. *Tick. Tock. Tick. Tock.*

Just one problem. Her alarm clock was electric.

BONG!

Carol's eyes popped open and she sat straight up in bed. She felt strange, disconnected, as if part of her was wide awake while another part slumbered on. But then, a cold meat loaf sandwich topped off with chocolate chip cookies, potato chips, jalapeño bean dip, and a quart of spiked eggnog would tend to do that to a person, she supposed.

Then she saw it: a hand snaking its way through the curtains at the foot of her bed. They were suddenly pulled aside, and just as suddenly, Carol realized she was dreaming.

She *had* to be dreaming. Because there stood Frank, bathed in an ethereal glow. He was dressed in some bizarre white outfit that looked suspiciously like the cap and gown she'd worn at her own college graduation.

"For crying out loud, Frank! You scared me!"

"I am the Ex of Xmas past!" he announced.

"Would you quit fooling around?" Carol demanded. "What the hell do you think you're doing?"

He waved his arms, making the sleeves of the robe flap dramatically. "I am here to help you."

"Ha! More likely you wanted to help yourself to a feel while I was sleeping! How did you get into my bedroom?"

Frank came around to the side of the bed, some sort of foggy vapor roiling and billowing around him with each step. As he approached her, Carol felt a distinct chill—and the first tingle of real fear at the back of her neck. His expression was grim.

"Stop being such a bitch and listen, Carol. I am here for your welfare. It's not much of a treat for me, either, you know."

"Then leave!"

"Not until you've seen what I have to show you."

Carol's eyes narrowed. "Frank, if you don't have any clothes on under that gown, you're dead meat."

"I told you. I am the Ex of Xmas past!"

"So you're a spirit, huh?" She was wrong. This wasn't a dream. It was a nightmare. "That would be a lot easier to believe if you weren't trying to peek down my nightie, Frank. Pretty strange behavior for an apparition."

"You'll believe in me soon. It's time to take a peek into your past." He reached out to her. "Take my hand."

She shook her head. "No way."

"Just take my hand, dammit! We don't have all night."

"You mean you can't suspend time?" He glowered at her. She grabbed his hand and held it. "Now what?"

"Close your eyes and listen."

Carol didn't like the idea. But she did it. In fact, she was suddenly having a hard time keeping her eyes open. What she heard was the sound that had awakened her, only now it seemed to be making her sleepy. There was a voice, too, deep and oddly soothing, trying to tell her something. Something about time. She leaned back against her pillows, listening.

Tick. Tock. Tick. Tock.

22

Carol was sitting cross-legged on the floor, gazing up at the Christmas tree. She'd dragged her mother and father all over Denver to pick it out, as usual. And as usual, she thought it was the most beautiful one in town. More.

"It's the perfectest tree in the whole world!"

"Most perfect, honey," her father corrected mildly.

She nodded. The most perfect tree on the most perfect day. Other children her age were unhappy now that Christmas was over, she knew, but Carol still felt good, even though all her presents had been opened. The one she valued the most was in the garage, a brand-new, bright-green two-wheeler, her first that came without training wheels attached. She was growing up! And that was the best present of all.

But of course, Uncle Fred was due any minute now, and he always had the topper. That's why she was sitting by the tree, trying to calm down. What she felt like doing was running all over the house; but if she did, her mother would cut off her sugar cookies. So there she sat, gazing at the tree, imagining a secret world among the multicolored lights and tinsel-strewn branches.

One of the ornaments was an intricately crafted little house, with a snow-covered gable roof and a big bay window to one side of its tiny door. This, too, had been a gift from Uncle Fred, but before she was born.

Carol scooted closer so she could peer through that window. There was a teeny-weeny light inside the house, on the ceiling, right where a real light would be. Below that was an itsy-bitsy family: a mommy, a daddy, and two children. They were all holding hands, looking at a Christmas tree just like the one she was sitting under right now.

What if there was a house ornament on that tree, too, with a family inside it, looking at a tree that had an ornament on it and . . .

"Whew!" Carol exclaimed, leaning back on her elbows.

Her mother looked up from her knitting. "What's wrong?"

"Just thinkin'."

"About what?"

She didn't have the words. "When's Uncle Fred coming?"

"Soon, dear. It's snowing out, you know."

Carol sighed and got up to look out the living-room window, trying to focus on each big flake that came swirling down from the dark sky. "I hope he hurries."

"I hope he chose something more appropriate this year," Edna Applegate said quietly. "Cap pistols! What kind of gift was that for a young lady? Why not a doll, or some clothes?"

Tom Applegate chuckled. "Carol liked 'em well enough."

"Go ahead and laugh," she said with a disdainful sniff. "You weren't the one who had to field all those phone calls. The neighbors thought we'd let a commando loose on them."

"Now, Edna. It wasn't that bad. Carol just has a very active and creative imagination, that's all," Tom said, smiling proudly. "It's worth a few irate neighbors."

"Humph! I'd trade some of that imagination for a bit of proficiency in math, thank you very much."

"He's here!" Carol squealed gleefully, pointing out the window as a car rolled to a stop in the Applegate's snowy driveway. She ran to the front door, not even hearing her mother chastise her. After grasping the knob in her small hands, she pulled open the door and yelled out at him. "Merry Christmas, Uncle Fred!"

"Merry Christmas!" he called back.

Carol hopped from foot to foot, impatiently waiting for him to climb the steps to the door. When he was inside, he bent over and held out his arms. She jumped into them and he straightened, holding her against him.

He bussed her cheek. "How's my favorite niece?"

"Fine," Carol replied, suddenly shy.

When she pictured Santa Claus, she saw Uncle Fred in a funny red suit. The hair on his head was so blond it was almost white, as was the bushy beard on his chin, and his blue eyes sparkled merrily just like in the story. When he laughed, his big tummy shook beneath her. Carol kissed him on the cheek, giggling as his whiskers tickled her face.

"Put that child down, Fred!" Edna exclaimed. "She's getting too big for that back of yours to handle."

Uncle Fred did put her down, but he was still smiling. "She is getting to be an armful, isn't she?" He winked at her. "I'll bet I know what you want!"

Carol nodded, so excited she couldn't speak.

"Let's see now," he said, patting the pockets of his long wool houndstooth check coat. "I know I had it somewhere."

"Stop teasing!" Carol cried.

He pulled a long box out of his inside pocket and gave it to her. "There you go!"

"Thank you!"

She started to run into the living room, but he called her back. "Wait! Here's another one!"

"Fred, you shouldn't have," Tom told him, helping him off with his coat. "She gets plenty as it is."

"The second one isn't much. Just something for her to practice on."

Edna didn't like the sound of that. "Practice

on? Fred, if that's some kind of noisy instrument—"

"Shh! I want to see her face!"

They went into the living room and sat down, watching Carol as she dropped to her knees near the tree to open her gifts. The long box made an interesting clinking sound when she shook it; she decided to save that for last. The other present was a heavy, solid rectangle about the size of her foot. It didn't make any noise at all. She tore the brightly colored paper off and stared at it, puzzled.

Uncle Fred was laughing fit to burst. "Ho! It's a block of wood, little one! Red oak. Open the other and you'll understand."

Her parents were on the edge of their seats, watching. Edna looked worried. Uncle Fred's expression was every bit as full of anticipation as Carol's.

Beneath the gift wrapping was a box, also wood, but smooth and highly polished. It had a little clasp on one edge. Carol opened it, her eyes growing wide. Inside, nestled in forest-green velvet, was a set of woodworking knives, their blades and ebony handles gleaming.

"For God's sake, Fred!" Edna exclaimed angrily. "She'll cut all her little fingers off!"

Her father was uncertain. "Gee, Fred, I don't know . . ."

Uncle Fred waved Carol over. "Come here, little one."

She did so, still staring at the knives with big blue eyes. There was an odd feeling inside her, not unlike the one she'd had when she was looking at the house ornament: the feeling of being overwhelmed by possibilities.

"They're so pretty!"

"And so sharp!" Uncle Fred told her softly. "These aren't playthings, Carol. They're tools. You're not to use them on anything except that block of wood until you know what you're doing, and not even that unless I or your father and mother are around to watch you. Do you understand?"

Carol looked up at him, the pride of responsibility welling up within her. She nodded solemnly. "Yes, sir."

"I have a book coming in the mail. When it arrives, I'll help you read it, so you can learn how to carve all sorts of beautiful things. Right now I think you ought to put those in a safe place. Okay?"

"Yes, sir."

"She'll cut her fingers off!" Edna Applegate repeated, wringing her hands fretfully.

But her father was satisfied. "Thank your Uncle Fred, honey, then go on up and get ready for bed."

"Thank you so much!" After gently closing the wooden box, she then put her arms around his neck and hugged him. "I'll be ever so careful!"

He smiled at her. "I know you will, little one. Now, quick as a bunny, do what your father says and I'll come tell you a story."

"A story!"

Carol kissed her father and mother good night. She almost started to dash to her room, but remembered her promise in the nick of time and walked instead, holding the woodworking tools in front of her as she would a carton of eggs.

At her age, there wasn't a safer, more sacrosanct place in the world than her underwear drawer. She stole one last peek at the knives, then put them away.

After she'd brushed her teeth and slipped on her pink flannel nightgown, Carol climbed into bed, waiting for Uncle Fred. The minute he came through her bedroom door, she made sure he knew his faith was not misplaced.

"I put them in the drawer with my undies!"

Uncle Fred chuckled. "Well, now! That's as careful as careful can be, isn't it?" He sat down on the bed next to her, pulling the covers up to her chin. "There."

"Can I build a house?"

He arched his pale-blond eyebrows. "A house?"

"Like the one on our tree."

"Oh. Certainly! But that takes a lot of skill. You'll have to practice and practice, then practice some more."

"I will, Uncle Fred!"

"All right, then. Because if you can do that, the sky's the limit. You could even be a famous artist some day, little one," he told her. "Ready for your story?"

Carol wiggled down farther into bed, nodding. She looked at his kind face, bathed in the soft glow of her bedside lamp. As always at Christmas, she felt as if there were magic in the air, glimmering all around her.

"Once upon a time, there was a beautiful castle in the mountains, high up in the clouds. A handsome prince lived there, with his lovely princess. She had long blond hair and pale-blue eyes, the envy of all the land. The princess loved her prince, and he loved her in return, with all his heart and soul. They were very happy together, sharing their hopes and dreams, waiting for the day when fate would bring them a family of their own.

"As often happened in that long-ago time, however, one day a mysterious stranger came to the little mountain kingdom. Though he walked boldly and carried his head high, all around him could tell he was up to mischief . . ."

Carol closed her eyes, listening more to the sound of his voice than the words. It was a story he had told before, with variations, but that didn't mean she was tired of it. In fact, it was comforting, a tale of love and glory that she could be certain would end happily, send her off to dreamland with a smile on her lips.

She dreamed of this and that, houses in the sky and the vague shape of her future, visions that seemed silly when remembered from the distance of an adult perspective. But the dreams of childhood can be powerful too, can exert a control that lingers on, far past the days of pigtails and bikes without training wheels.

Carol carried her dreams into the future, and as she grew up tall and strong, so did they.

Tick. Tock. Tick. Tock.

23

Carol nervously fingered the hand-carved wooden dove that hung on a chain around her neck. What was wrong with her? Why couldn't she just relax and enjoy it?

Her folks weren't due home until eleven, and it was only nine. Even though it was Christmas vacation, she'd done the daily hour of algebra her mother insisted upon without being told. And she was old enough to drive now, for heaven's sake! What was the big deal about having a boy over to watch TV?

Okay, it was against the rules. Maybe they didn't even know what program was on. So what if the boy had his tongue halfway down her throat. Carol liked Jerry and she liked to kiss. No harm in an innocent kiss.

Just when she'd started to convince herself everything was fine, Jerry put his hand on her nylon-clad thigh, just below the hem of her skirt.

"Jerry . . ."

"Wow! Are your legs warm!"

His hand was warm too. The touch of it made her tingle inside. It felt good. *Too* good. "Stop that!" Carol exclaimed, batting his hand away, making a game of it.

"Tease."

Jerry started to kiss her again. That was more like it. Frenching made her tingle too, but in a way she felt she could control. Carol had a more experienced friend who had told her that once you started serious petting, things could get out of control in a hurry. She took Jerry's hand in hers so she could keep track of it.

He had on some kind of woodsy aftershave, or maybe it was cologne; she didn't know if Jerry shaved yet. He was a year younger but in her class, one of those lucky few to whom schoolwork had always come easy. That was how they'd met. Carol was struggling and he'd offered to help.

Unfortunately, she was beginning to get the feeling he was advanced beyond his years in other ways as well. She had his left hand firmly in her grasp, but he'd slipped his right behind her and was now resting it lightly on her breast. Carol leaned back on the couch, trapping his arm.

"Come on, Carol," he urged softly. "You'll like it."

That was the problem. She thought she probably would.

"No."

Somewhere along the path of his education, Jerry must have heard that when a girl said no, she actually meant yes. He managed to regain possession of his other hand and put it on her thigh again, this time *under* her skirt. An involuntary moan escaped her lips.

"Wow! You've got sensitive skin, huh?"

"Stop it!" Carol pushed his hand away, more firmly now, not playing around. "I mean it, Jerry. Why can't we just kiss and hold each other? I like that."

"Relax," he said, removing his hand.

Carol breathed a rather hoarse sigh of relief. But it was only a momentary ploy. Now his hand was on one of her breasts, massaging her through her blouse, making her feel things she never had before. She moaned again, her pulse quickening. Jerry urgently put his mouth to hers, moving his hand to her other breast.

He seemed to want to touch her so badly. Carol was confused and uncertain of what she wanted. That Jerry was getting such enjoyment from her body excited her, but her ingrained sense of morality told her it was wrong. Stiffening, she pushed his hand away again.

Then he glided his hand up her thigh beneath her skirt and touched her *there.* Though Carol was no stranger to arousal, this was the first time she'd felt it with someone else in the driver's seat. She closed her eyes, gasping for breath. Her friend had been right; things were quickly getting out of control.

Carol gave him a hard shove and stood up, whirling to face him. "I said no! You'd better leave now, Jerry."

Jerry got to his feet. For a moment, Carol's attention was captured by the bulge that strained the front of his pants. Then she looked at his face. He was grinning.

"Your parents won't be home for hours yet. Let's go to your room and get it on." Jerry reached for her hand.

She stepped back. "I told you to leave!"

"Wow! Are you . . ." His jaw went slack. "You've never done it, have you?"

Color rose to her cheeks, hot and embarrassing. "I'm not that kind of girl!"

"Yeah, right," he said, laughing at her. "Next you'll tell me you're saving yourself for marriage."

"And what's wrong with that?" Carol demanded.

"Christ! What a prude! Grow up, Applegate!"

"Me! You're the one who's immature, playing with sex like it was some kind of game!" She put her hands on her hips. "I want it to be with someone special, someone I love. *That's* being grown-up, Jerry Fields! Now get out of my house!"

Still laughing, he grabbed his coat and left, slamming the door on his way out. Carol felt hurt, embarrassed, and knew she would be the brunt of many jokes when she went back to school next week.

But she also felt good inside. She had stood up for what she believed in. And held onto her dreams. Maybe it was naive to wait for a prince, but that didn't mean she had to settle for a toad.

Tick. Tock. Tick. Tock.

24

"Hey! Remember me?"

Carol opened her eyes. "Of course!"

"Then raise your hips a bit for me. Mmm! That's better!"

"Oh! I'll say!"

"You're so beautiful, Carol!"

She gazed up at him, smiling, stroking the smooth skin of his sides with her fingertips. He was beautiful too. A lock of his thick brown hair had fallen into his eyes, blue eyes that gazed into hers with so much desire she felt giddy.

"Don't tease me, Billy! I'm about to explode!"

"You're the tease!" Moaning, he lowered himself onto her again, putting one hand beneath her gyrating hips to guide himself deeper into her. "That's it," he whispered in a hoarse, coaxing voice. "Such a good student!"

Carol laughed wickedly. "Such a good teacher!" She ran the tip of her tongue between his lips, matching his rhythm. His body started to shudder. "Oh! Oh, yes! Now!"

She shuddered too, over and over, writhing beneath the delicious pressure of each strong, sure penetration. He was good, better than good, tender and gentle yet so dominant in his masculine needs. Because he always made certain she met those needs completely, making love to him made her feel like the powerful one. Bill Peale had taught her, and she had learned, how sweet it was to give pleasure by taking her own.

They lay side by side, panting and laughing, holding each other tight. When at last their breathing slowed, he rolled onto his back. Carol propped herself on one elbow, gazing at his face. She knew perfectly well what made their lovemaking so ardent and important. She was in love.

She kissed him on the tip of his nose. "Silly Billy. What's that frown for? Didn't I satisfy you? Maybe you need a little more?" she asked softly, reaching for him.

"God, no!" He laughed, taking her hand. "Not yet, anyway. I was just thinking."

"About what?"

"What else? Graduation," Bill replied. "It's just a little over six months away, you know."

Carol sighed. "Yeah. I've been thinking a lot about that myself lately. I mean, not graduating, really. But what comes after. Scary, isn't it?"

"No! It's exciting!"

"For you, maybe. You made the dean's list last term. I was lucky to squeak by my accounting final."

"Still . . ." He trailed off, idly stroking the back of her hand with his thumb. "There's a big world out there, Carol. I guess it is a bit scary. But think of the challenges waiting for us."

She rolled onto her back as well, looking at the ceiling. Bill's studio apartment wasn't much bigger than her dorm room, nor was it located in the most savory part of town. But it was their love nest and as such it seemed a palace to Carol.

Unfortunately, it also reminded her of something.

"Right," she said. "Challenges like finding a place to live and going full time at work. Paying rent and utility bills and buying groceries. Budgeting and saving. I'm ecstatic." Then she chuckled. "Listen to me! Sorry to be such a downer. Must be postcoital depression or something."

"That's okay. It's important to think about that stuff. Helps you get your head straight, put your priorities in order."

Bill released her hand and reached down to pull the bed covers up over them. They'd been warm enough before, but now the late December wind trickling through the ill-fitting apartment windows was giving them both goosebumps. He pulled her against him and wrapped his arms around her from behind, cupping her breasts.

She felt perfect in his arms. Bill was her first lover, or at least the first she'd ever gone all the way with. Her girlfriends had called her crazy for waiting so long, and maybe they had a point. In many ways, Carol thought of these love lessons as the best part of her college education. Not that she was preoccupied with sex, necessarily. But it was great. So was this new feeling that Bill had awakened in her, way past the infatuations she'd had to date.

Love. Now that was a priority. If you were in love, all the rest of it fell into place, didn't it? "Bill?"

"Hmm?"

"What are your priorities?" she asked.

"Staying on the dean's list. Graduating. Living life to the fullest." He nibbled on her neck. "And making love to you!"

"Be serious!"

"But I am serious." After sliding down on the bed a little, Bill lifted her leg atop his and slowly entered her. "See?"

Carol groaned, burying her face in a pillow as he thrust into her again and again, making the bedsprings squeak. His neighbors probably hated them, but she didn't care; to her the sound was unbelievably erotic and she reveled in it, as she enjoyed every passionate moan that escaped his lips. She loved him, loved the feel of him pulsing inside her.

They cried out together in joyful pleasure. Life! How perfect it seemed at twenty-one! Young and strong, full of themselves and their possibilities, so certain of their desires.

"Mercy!" Carol pleaded. "If you wear me out, I can't go shopping for your present later, can I?" He kissed the tips of her breasts, chuckling throatily. "Stop that! Silly Billy! You've used me all up!"

"Carol Climax? Never!"

Blushing from head to toe, she bounded out of bed, away from his tempting grasp. The floor was cold on her bare feet. Bill whistled at her as she sashayed into the bathroom, and again when she emerged awhile later. He was pulling on his jeans, but she still didn't trust him not to pounce on her again, so she quickly slipped into her clothes as well.

"Hey," he said softly. "Come here."

"I don't think so!"

Bill grabbed her hand and pulled her into his lap. "I just wanted to hold you for a second. Have I told you how wonderful you are today?"

"Today? Let's see . . . only about ten times," she told him, hugging him fiercely. "Oh, Bill! I love you so much!"

"Ouch! Easy, girl, you'll break my ribs!" He stood up with Carol still in his arms, then set her gently on her feet. "I have something I need to tell you, Carol," he said, taking her hand. "I was going to wait a few months, but I think maybe I'd better do it now. You know, graduation is getting so close and there are plans to make."

She felt her heart give a little stutter-step in her chest. He was going to ask her to marry him! Visions of a June wedding danced through her mind, along with the more down-to-earth thoughts an accounting student like herself was destined to have. Two incomes! They'd both be entry level of course, her as a bookkeeper, Bill in data processing. But if they were frugal for a few years they might even be able to save enough for a down payment on some land.

And some day build a house in the mountains. That was her dream. A place where she could allow the creative part of herself she'd suppressed for so long to emerge at last.

"Carol?"

She laughed. "Sorry! Just daydreaming. Go ahead, Bill. You don't have to stand on ceremony with me!"

"God! You're such a special woman." He looked deep into her eyes and said, "I joined the navy, Carol."

Carol blinked, her visions of wedding cake and snowy peaks gone in a puff of smoke. "What?"

"My hitch starts three weeks after I graduate. I'll be in San Diego for basic, hard to tell after that. I'm going in for computer training, maybe submarine duty, and in a couple of years—"

"Wait!" This was all too much for Carol. She was still trying to assimilate the first thing he'd said. "You joined the navy?"

Bill laughed. "Yeah, I know, you probably think I fell for all that malarky about seeing the world. And maybe I did a little bit. But it's hard to jump right into the computer field without any experience, and the recruiter said I'd get plenty of that if I make the grade."

"I don't know what to say."

She really didn't. Bill had come into her life suddenly, and there had been such an intense attraction between them that they had become lovers almost at once. They hadn't done much talking about the future, but he was part of her life now. How could he just leave her?

Bill was smiling. "I want you to come with me, Carol."

"Come with you?" Now she was really confused. "I don't want to join the navy!"

"That's not what I meant," he told her, laughing at her stunned expression. "I'll eventually be assigned to a home base somewhere. When I am, I could send for you."

"Excuse me?"

"Send for you. Help you move," he explained. "You could get a little apartment near the base or something. I could even help you out until you found a job."

Whatever it was he wanted, it certainly wasn't her hand in marriage. "I can't just pick up and leave!" she exclaimed. "I haven't been spending all my weekends at the welding shop for fun, you know. I've been learning their system. Once I graduate and go full time, I can work my way into a position to oversee their accounting department. You're asking me to throw all that away and start over from scratch."

He frowned. "I thought you said you loved me?"

"I do! But I don't recall hearing an awful lot of commitment in those plans of yours. Don't you love me?"

The silence was deafening, an answer in itself. Then Bill said, "Gosh, Carol. I thought we should take it easy to begin with. You know. Live together for a while. I mean, we're young, not too sure of what we want out of life yet."

Carol stared at him, perhaps seeing him clearly for the first time. It gave her a sinking feeling deep inside. But in a way she was grateful; this was the most important lesson he'd ever taught her. Don't mistake sex for love.

"Speak for yourself, Bill," she said. "I do know what I want. And I'm getting a pretty good idea of what you want now too. A nice, convenient relationship you can walk in and out of whenever you please." She turned away from him. "I have dreams and aspirations of my own, you know. But it's obvious you don't care about those. It's also obvious we should stop seeing each other. There's no future in it."

"But there could be, Carol! Give it a chance. Give *us* a chance. We won't know until we try."

"Stop it!" Carol demanded, facing him again. "Be honest. Why are you joining the navy in the first place?"

"To expand my horizons, I guess. I'll get the training I need to better myself, and at the same time I'll get to see lots of interesting new things, different places."

"And different faces too, right?"

He shrugged. "Sure."

"Where do I fit in?" she asked. "Am I supposed to be the familiar face from home that'll see you through until you find someone else?"

"No! I do care for you, Carol. I just . . . I'm

not ready to make the kind of commitment you're talking about. Not yet. Maybe in a few years, when I've seen and done more."

"And you want me to wait patiently until then?" She shook her head sadly. "I already love you. I'd happily live in a little apartment with you. I suppose I could get used to waiting for you to get shore leave so we could be together. But not as a sometime girlfriend you might learn to love. I have plans too, and what you're offering me isn't even a compromise."

Now he got angry. "Stop trying to trap me!"

"I'm not! I'm just telling you that love is much higher on my list of priorities than it is on yours," she said, trying to sound so adult when inside she felt like a wounded little girl. "So I'm going to do what you can't seem to bring yourself to do: Say good-bye. Our dreams are different, Bill. You go see the world. I'll find someone else to share mine."

Carol walked out of his apartment, tears running down her face. She never looked back, and he never came after her. Her first love. Her first broken heart. In time she forgot them both. But then, she'd forgotten a lot of things.

Tick. Tock. Tick. Tock.

25

Flash bulbs popped. Her mother sobbed. Carol opened her eyes, realizing she had just kissed her husband for the first time. Oh, God! She was Carol Case now!

They strolled back down the aisle hand in hand, going through a gauntlet of smiles and happy tears. Carol gripped Frank's arm, feeling so much emotion inside she was certain she would float away if he wasn't there to hold on to her. He beamed at her, laughing as they ducked a hail of gaily colored rice. Once safely ensconced in the limo that would whisk them to the reception, Frank kissed her again.

"I love you, Mrs. Case," he said somberly.

"And I love you, Mr. Case."

Then he grinned. "You know what I want to do?"

"Me too," Carol assured him, her eyes bright with excitement. They'd made love before, but not as man and wife. There was something so significant about the idea, almost as if their previous intimacy didn't count. "But we have to endure the reception first."

Frank groaned and rolled his eyes. "I know.

Did you see my mom? She could've filled a bucket."

"Same with mine. Dad will probably have to stop and change his shirt."

They laughed, holding hands and hugging each other, feeling like royalty as the chauffeur-driven limousine rolled along in silent, stately grace. The streets were decorated for the holidays, sparkling garlands and tiny, twinkling lights, adding festive cheer to their happiness.

"It was nice of your folks to spring for our honeymoon," Frank said. "I'll pay them back as soon as that deal in Craig goes through."

"Don't be silly. They wanted to do it. It'll be so romantic! Christmastime in the mountains!"

Frank leaned over and nibbled on her neck. "Yeah, but I don't think we'll get much skiing in, do you?"

"I guess not," she agreed, blushing. "We'll at least have to take one run, though. On the same slope where we met. I'll try not to crash into you this time."

"Feel free. It was worth it." He brought her hand to his lips. "Mmm! I can hardly wait!"

The reception was a blur of voices, half-remembered conversations, and seemingly endless ceremony. Cutting the cake together. Being toasted by relatives they hadn't seen in years. Dancing with everyone but each other. It was odd how the whole thing seemed designed to keep them apart as much as possible. When they did steal a moment, they were always aware of being carefully observed, judged, and graded as to their suitability for one another.

"Don't they make a lovely couple?"

"Happy as larks too. Just look at 'em."

"Frank is quite handsome, don't you think?"

"Slim, trim, and debonair. That beard makes him look so distinguished. And Carol! All brides are beautiful, but she positively glows!"

Carol nearly died of embarrassment when she discovered that Uncle Fred had brought the little metal casting she'd sent him for Christmas and was showing it to everyone he could grab. It was pitiful in her opinion, a fawn taking its first steps on spindly legs, something she'd done in one of her night sculpture classes to prove competence in a certain technique. She knew he'd get a kick out of it, but hadn't expected him to boast about it at her wedding!

Maybe it was appropriate, though. That sculpture was just like her, a newborn heading off in a fresh, scary but exciting direction, just as she was about to set off upon a new life full of uncertainty and promise.

Keeping the books for the welding shop had turned into a bear of a job now that they'd expanded. Her art classes were the only things that kept her sane. Over the past three years, teachers had commented on her talent, and at long last she was starting to believe them. That only made it all the more difficult to keep plodding along the safe, sure road she was on. But she was prepared to work hard to make her dreams come true.

And now she had someone to share them with. Frank loved the mountains too, albeit more for their mineral value than their beauty. This deal he was working on could be their ticket to freedom, that home in the clouds and her chance to see just how talented she really was.

Their eyes met across the crowded banquet hall and Carol felt a thrill run through her. It was time to change out of their finery and leave. One final embarrassing moment, as they slipped out the door followed by sly winks and bawdy comments, then a frenzied escape in Frank's graffiti-covered truck. Finally they lost their honking entourage and got rid of the clattering cans. Married.

Now for the consummation!

It was the longest drive of Carol's life. The weather was cold and snowy, especially once they left the city and got into the mountains, but that wasn't the only reason the truck windows were steaming up. They were sitting so close she was sure no one could tell which one of them was driving. On occasion neither of them was, until they almost slipped into a ditch and forced themselves to keep their hands off each other. At last, they arrived.

"Some day I'll carry you over the threshold of a house up here," Frank said as he lifted her into his arms.

Carol didn't know if the ski resort even had a bridal suite, and was quite sure her parents couldn't have afforded it in any case, but their room was absolutely perfect as far as she was concerned. It had a kitchenette, a separate sitting room with a big stone fireplace, and a gorgeous view of the snow-covered peaks.

And a great big bed. As soon as Frank put her down, she kicked off her shoes and jumped into the middle of it. "God! I thought we'd never get here!" Carol exclaimed.

"We almost didn't, you crazy blond vixen!"

"Look who's talking, you bearded beast! Come here and put me out of my misery!"

Their clothing flew in every direction as they rolled around on the bed undressing each other. After miles and miles of longing glances and teasing caresses, neither of them was in any mood for foreplay. Carol pounced on him as he lay on his back, lowering herself down onto his rock-hard masculinity. It only took a few quick movements of her hips to bring them both to a shattering orgasm.

But they were far from satisfied. Pinning her beneath him, Frank took her with such passion that she had to grab the covers to keep from rolling off the bed, gasping at each powerful thrust. Carol hoped the suite was as soundproof as it was beautiful, because she couldn't stop herself from crying out at the unbelievable joy she felt at being so totally possessed by him. Love, married love, the complete fulfillment of her every sensual and emotional desire!

They showered together afterward, their mutual need temporarily sated, but as they soaped each other's bodies from head to toe it returned full force. Frank lifted her and she wrapped her legs around his torso, guiding him into her amid the hot, stinging spray. The position proved too much for them both, and they ended up on all fours in the bathtub for the ultimate finish.

They had reservations in a fancy restaurant for dinner, and the food was undoubtedly marvelous, but neither of them really concentrated on it. When they were through they went dancing, heedless of the knowing smiles around them as they moved against one another in a sensual *pas de deux.*

Walking back to their hotel through the snow, bathed in moonlight and the cozy glow of frosted Christmas decorations, Carol held him tight and tried to grasp the enormity of her emotions. Her love for Frank was overwhelming. Perhaps because she was an only child, she had never been one of those women who constantly thought of babies. Now, however, her maternal feelings were coming on strong. Their financial situation wouldn't be solid enough to have children right away, but as soon as possible she wanted to start a family, add another glorious layer to the fabric of her dreams.

A bottle of champagne was waiting for them when they got back to their room. They sat before a roaring fire, drinking silent toasts to their love and just holding each other. At last the fire burned low and they went to bed, sleeping blissfully in one another's arms.

Carol cooked breakfast for him the next day,

puttering around in the kitchenette, playing her new role to the hilt. Of course, she doubted many wives cooked in a frilly teddy and high heels. As she'd planned, it proved too much for Frank to bear. He scarcely made it through the meal.

"I'll help you wash the dishes," he said, coming up behind her as she stood at the sink.

She moaned as he put his arms around her and began massaging her breasts. "I don't think that's going to be much help, dear."

"To hell with 'em, then."

Before Carol knew what was happening, Frank was lifting her onto the countertop. But she quickly figured out what he had in mind. With her legs draped over his shoulders and the teddy dangling from one ankle, she arched her back to accept the delicious teasing of his tongue. When she could stand no more, he took her right there on the counter, standing on tiptoe and feeling her high heels digging into his buttocks. The physical struggle was well worth the exciting reward of being so totally wicked and spontaneous.

Their honeymoon was perfect, three days in heaven. They made love whenever and wherever the mood grabbed them, ate when they needed energy, and slept when they could no longer keep up the pace. A quick outing on the ski slope to reenact the day they met left Carol stunned by the role fate had played in her joy.

"What if I'd just fallen down instead of plowing into you?" she asked him, standing beneath a bower of snow blanketed pine trees. "What if—"

"Shh!" Frank hugged her. "Don't question it. Just enjoy it. We were destined to be together."

Carol cherished that thought. Even when the honeymoon was over and they went back to their everyday existence, it all seemed so perfect, destined to happen.

Soon, though, she found out what fate had really had in mind when it had thrown Frank in front of her that day. What had begun with unbelievable joy and passion ended obscured by acid bitterness. But they had been very much in love once. Carol had forgotten those feelings, just as she had forgotten the happiness that had preceded her first broken heart. Until now.

Tick. Tock. Tick. Tock.

26

Carol raised her head from Sean's chest and gazed up into his compassionate green eyes. "I'm sorry. I'm getting your shirt all wet," she said, wiping her cheeks with the tissue he'd given her.

"It'll dry." They were standing in Sean's living room, Carol wrapped in his big, strong arms while she had wept tears of bitter anger and frustration. "Feeling better now?"

Nodding, she replied, "Yes, thanks." Her voice was hoarse. "I bet I look just awful, though."

"You're always beautiful. Go blow your nose and splash some cold water on your face and you'll be good as new."

She sighed and pulled away from him, suddenly realizing how intimate their position seemed. Other than an innocent good-night kiss or two after what couldn't even be described as real dates, the only other time Carol had been this close to Sean O'Phaelan was at the amusement park in Denver that summer. He'd put his arms around her then too, but only to keep her slender form from slipping beneath the roller coaster's restraining bar.

How they'd laughed! And how embarrassed she'd been when Bobbi Cathecart kept making sly comments about how nice they looked together. But that position hardly compared to sobbing against his chest while he held her tight; and this situation was even more embarrassing.

She and Sean really didn't know each other all that well, but the moment he'd seen her walk through the door of The Naked Waitress, he had known something was wrong; and the moment she'd seen him, she'd started to cry, knowing he would rush to her side. Strange.

When she emerged from the bathroom a while later, Sean asked, "How about a nice, hot cup of tea?"

"That sounds great."

They went into the apartment's small kitchen. Carol sat down at a little table near the window while he made the tea. She smiled when he pulled a bottle of Irish whiskey from the cabinet above the sink and added a dollop of it to her cup. The first taste made her cough, but she quickly got accustomed to the heady brew.

"I'm sorry to bother you like this," Carol told him. "I'd just intended to come get a drink and cool off, before I went after the bastard and chopped him into pieces. I don't know what made me break down like that."

Sean patted her hand. "It's never a bother to

comfort a friend, Carol. And from what I've heard, you have every reason to want to trim a few pieces off your ex-husband," he assured her. "As for breaking down, it seems to me you've been holding something in for too long. Maybe it would help if you got it all off your chest."

Carol had told him she'd been married once and that it had ended badly. Whatever else he knew came from town gossip, most likely Bobbi Cathecart. Sean was right; she'd held it in for much too long.

Suddenly she wanted to talk, and Sean was a very good listener. He sat there, nodding and murmuring words of encouragement, as the whole sorry story poured forth from her in waves.

"So the turning point was the deal in Craig?" Sean asked.

She shrugged. Maybe it was the third cup of laced tea, but Carol was feeling more at ease with Sean than she'd felt with anyone for a long time. "I don't know. There were other things before that," she told him. "For instance, the man is a pig. Dirty clothes all over the house; never lifted a hand to help with anything. But after that deal he started drinking more and things got much, much worse."

"Because he didn't get enough money out of it?"

"I suppose. I eventually learned that failure wasn't new to Frank, but I guess this one hit him harder because he'd promised so many people so much, including me." Carol sipped at her tea. "Fool that I was at the time, though, I told him it was okay, that there would be other deals. How right I was; he'd already invested what little money he did get in yet another scheme, without even asking me."

"And that one?"

Carol pursed her lips and made a thumbs-down gesture. "In the toilet. It was a mining claim that turned out to be a share of nothing, and so the money was gone. That was when I started to get the feeling I'd made a big mistake."

"Everyone makes mistakes, Carol," Sean told her, his tone sympathetic.

"Sure, but you're supposed to learn from them. I didn't. Instead, I held on to my faith in him and gave him access to my own hard-earned savings, only to see them go toward equipment that never quite paid for itself or mineral rights that required still more equipment, all of which he would eventually sell for a pittance. Frank would just dust himself off, promise me the moon, then turn around and get into greater debt somewhere else."

Sean shook his head. "Sounds like a nasty habit, all right. Frank obviously chose the wrong profession," he said. "But in my opinion, his biggest failure was not realizing what a special woman he was married to."

"Right. Especially thick-headed."

"Stop it," Sean ordered gently. "You can't let what he did sour you like this. Yes, he's a bastard. Yes, you were taken in by him. But faith is admirable, not stupid; without it we have nothing."

"That's about what I had when Frank got done with me."

He ignored her bitter remark. "Take me for instance." Sean waved a hand, indicating the walls around them. "My father was disappointed when I decided not to go into his construction business, but he still had faith in me. That in turn gave me faith in myself. Of course, I suppose it helped that I decided to open a pub," he added with a wry grin. "As far as Dad's concerned, if I wasn't going to be a builder, tapping beer kegs was the next best thing."

Carol smiled. Sean could always make her smile. "You mean if you had your heart set on raising poodles or some such, he might have lost faith?"

"No. He might have come after me with a two-by-four and tried to beat some sense into me, but he still would have had faith," Sean replied. "That's what I mean. Frank's biggest mistake was not taking the support you gave him and using it to build a better life for you both."

"He tried, I guess," Carol admitted grudgingly. "But you're right. There came a time when it was obvious he should cut his losses and find a real job, something that would help me pay the bills instead of being the biggest hole in our budget. As it was, I had to grab every minute of overtime I could." She grimaced at the memory. "I was dog-tired all the time. We . . . Well, when I went to bed, it was to sleep and that's all. Frank blamed it on the art classes I refused to give up. We had some real screaming matches over that, but without those classes I would have gone stark raving mad."

Sean reached out and took her hand. "That's another reason you're so special. You held on to your dreams, even under all that pressure. Lord!" he exclaimed, his tone one of admiration. "I thought it took a lot of courage for me to abandon a sure thing and go into business for myself. You did it against odds that would've crushed me flat."

Carol squeezed his hand. "I doubt that, Sean. But it was awful. I kept my dreams in my heart, but in reality they had to fall by the wayside, held hostage by the day-to-day drain of Frank's. When I think of all the opportunities I missed!" Her voice was full of outrage. "I had lots of ideas; more than one of my teachers told me I could easily make money on them too. But I was working so hard for the welding shop chain that I seldom had time to create."

"I'm amazed you didn't kick him out long before you did. What stopped you?" Sean asked.

"Hell, I don't know. We'd only been married a little over a year. I thought things would get better, and my mother helped out in that department. To her credit, she had never been all that pleased with Frank. But to her, marriage is forever. She kept telling me to hold on, pointing to the hard times she and my dad had gone through. You know how parents can be."

"And how!" Sean agreed. "Take my mother. I love her like crazy, but I have just the opposite problem with her. Mom doesn't particularly care who I marry or how long it lasts, just so she gets some more grandchildren."

"But she already has them. Didn't you say that both your brothers and one of your sisters have kids?"

"Six all told," Sean replied. "So far. But she won't be happy until all of us are settled down and proving our fertility." He sighed. "It's not that I don't want a family. I do. But I've been in and out of enough no-win relationships to know what I want. I'll bide my time."

Carol was very much aware of his gaze upon her. She looked into his eyes, feeling something stir within her that she hadn't felt for a long time. Was he implying he wanted more than a friendly relationship with her? Was she actually considering the possibility herself?

She looked away, carefully quashing such thoughts. "In a way, I'm very glad Frank and I did have financial troubles right from the start. If we'd brought children into the mess we were headed for . . ." Carol trailed off, frowning. "I was so busy keeping us afloat that I must have managed to blind myself to what was happening. It seemed as if I woke up one day to find I was married to a total stranger I despised, a lazy, slovenly, beer-swilling wastrel who continued to think the next deal would solve all our problems."

"So you divorced him," Sean concluded.

Carol uttered a short, curt laugh. "Are you kidding? Not me. With all the crap he put me through, all the weight he was putting on, I wouldn't even let him near me anymore, but I still harbored a small hope something would magically change everything. And it did."

Money problems, animosity, no sex life. Sean figured he knew what had happened. "He started cheating on you?"

Her nod confirmed it. "I never caught him at it, but I could tell there was some other woman who didn't share my disdain for his lifestyle and appearance. That was the last straw." Carol's smile was bitter. "So I filed on him. Put the papers in one of the socks he left lying around and tacked it to the mantel on Christmas Eve."

Sean had to chuckle. "Nice touch. It's a wonder he didn't fight it, though, considering what a gravy train he'd found in you."

"You don't know Frank," Carol said. "It was fine with him. As far as he was concerned, a divorce was just a way he could live the way he wanted without me nagging him. He'd still drop by when the only other people who'd lend him money were threatening to break his legs. I should have let them. As of this Christmas, I will."

"Good for you."

His voice was soft, supportive, and full of a kindness she desperately needed. Carol suddenly realized that she and Sean had grown much closer than she'd thought over the past couple of years. "Thanks, Sean," she said. "You're a good friend." She glanced at her watch. "And here I am taking advantage of you! It's past closing time!"

"Maureen took care of it. And you can feel free to take advantage of me any time." He patted her hand, then released it and got to his feet. "Come on, I'll walk you."

"You don't—"

"I want to."

As they strolled along the icy sidewalk toward her house, Carol's arm naturally intertwined with his. She felt at peace by his side. "I like this town," she murmured.

"Me too. It's great to find home at last, isn't it?"

Home. "That's just the way I feel too. My house needs a lot of work and I need a new car; I could probably make more money elsewhere. Eventually I want to try to take my castings into national distribution. But I'll always want to live right here. This is my dream."

"And mine. To me, it's worth a bit less money and the occasional inconvenience of a small town to have this beauty around me. Living in Tithe is like having a built-in family, one I've decided I want to add to some day."

Carol nodded slightly but didn't say anything. The thought did tiptoe ever so softly across her mind now and again. But that was too far ahead for her to think right now. She'd made her Christmas change for one year by at last telling Frank to take a flying leap.

She and Sean had much in common. Maybe some day Carol would feel secure enough emotionally to find out how much. But not just yet. That would have to wait for other Christmas seasons, other years.

Still, when they stepped onto her porch, she had the sudden urge to invite him inside. But that wouldn't be wise. This was a very vulnerable moment for her.

Sean seemed in tune with her thoughts. "I'm glad you felt able to confide in me tonight, Carol." He bent and touched his lips lightly to her cheek. "Good night."

"Wait."

He turned to her again, his eyebrows arched. "Yes?"

"Sean . . . thank you."

Carol put her arms around him, hugging him tight. Before she realized what was happening, she was kissing him, deeply, hungry for the taste of him. When at last their lips parted, all she could do was look at him, stunned at the barrier she had just crossed.

Though just as stunned, Sean at least was able to speak. "Would you go to dinner with me tomorrow night?"

She nodded. "I-I'd like that."

Smiling, Sean turned again and headed down the driveway, whistling a happy tune. Carol let herself into her house and leaned against the closed door.

"Oh, God," she muttered. "What have I done?"

A real date. With a man she was no longer thinking of as merely a friend. Something had just happened between them; a spark had kindled to life and now smoldered gently within her. Desire, a need to have a man in her life again, Carol couldn't quite put her finger on it. Nor could she deny the feeling. But since it was among those she had kept carefully locked out for so many years, even this subtle change in their relationship scared her.

What really frightened her, though, was that deep down inside, she knew precisely what was happening. After all, she'd gone through it at least twice before. They were taking those first tentative steps toward falling in love.

The first blush of romance. How sweet it felt!

And yet Carol knew they didn't have a chance, all because of a man who had taken everything she had to give and crumpled it in his grimy, unfeeling hands. Perhaps if she had stood up for herself before today, made Frank leave her alone after the divorce so her wounds could heal, she might be a different woman.

As it was, for all its tender sweetness, this newborn love was doomed before it had even begun.

Tick. Tock. Tick. Tock.

27

The first thing Carol saw when she opened her eyes was Frank bending over her. He had a wary, puzzled expression on his face. "You okay?" he asked.

Carol made a grab for his throat. "Damn you!"

"Hey!" The Ex of Xmas past jumped backward from the bed, waving his arms for balance. "Take it easy! I'm sorry if you don't like what you're seeing, but it's the truth. You can't strangle the truth, Carol."

"I'll give you truth!" she cried, jumping out of bed and advancing on him. "Why did you have to turn out to be such a lazy bastard? Why couldn't you have worked as hard for me as I did for you? Why didn't you leave me alone so I could get over the pain, instead of constantly reminding me of what I'd lost? I'm going to tear your head off for what you did to me, Frank!"

"Now, Carol—" She lunged at him again. Frank dashed to the end of the bed, white robe flapping around his ankles. "You're missing the point," he said quickly, using the bedcurtains to fend off her blows. "You have to put that anger aside and concentrate on your other feelings. You say you don't need love. Now you remember a time when it meant everything to you. It can be that way again, Carol. You've seen what's in your heart. Let it out!"

"Never!" Carol tackled him, knocking him back onto the bed. She grabbed a pillow and stuffed it against his face. "Never again, do you hear? Never!"

"Help!" Frank cried.

Tick! Tock! Tick! Tock!

28

Carol woke up to find she was on her hands and knees in the middle of the bed, fists clenched into a pillow. She lifted it. Nothing.

"Frank?"

Silence. She drew the bedcurtains open a crack and took a peek. While she slept, the storm must have shifted in another direction, because moonlight now filtered through the window, filling the room with a strange, ethereal glow.

So it had been a dream. Just a dream. Shivers wracked her and she climbed back beneath the covers, pulling them up to her chin. Damn that stupid eggnog! Damn sentimental Christmas movies! And double damn men!

You can't strangle the truth.

She closed her eyes tight, shaking her head. But she couldn't get rid of the truth that way, either. Whether a dream or a visitation or a cold meat loaf sandwich, the memories Carol had just relived were true, and she knew it. No matter how hard she tried to forget, her love for Bill and Frank had been real. There *was* a time when love had meant everything to her. She and Sean *had* fallen in love. And love felt very good indeed.

BONG! BONG!

"Oh, God!" Carol groaned. "Not again!"

The bedcurtains were pulled aside. "I am the Ex of Xmas present!"

Carol's eyes went wide as saucers. It was Sean, dressed all in Christmas green. "Dammit! Would you guys quit messing with my head? If you have something to say, just say it and get out so I can get some sleep!"

"So you still don't believe?" He shook his head, making the little bell on his green stocking cap jingle merrily. Like Frank, however, his expression was serious. "Well, before this night is out, you will," Sean assured her. "Take my hand."

She crossed her arms. "No."

"I am the Ex of Xmas present, here to show you the joy of others on this day. Now, take my hand!"

This wasn't right. She hadn't gotten around to telling him they were through. He wasn't an ex anything yet. There was no reason for him to be playing this role unless . . . unless all these things really were a product of her own wildly creative imagination!

Oh, God! The confusion and pressure had finally gotten to her, overloaded a circuit breaker in her brain! She was going mad! "Help me, Sean!" she cried. "I'm losing my marbles! Please tell me this is something you cooked up."

"Take my hand!"

Carol grabbed the hand he held out to her, squeezing it fiercely, drawing comfort from him though she could tell by the look on his face he had precious little comfort in store for her. She closed her eyes, listening as she had before.

Tick. Tock. Tick. Tock.

29

"A toast!" David Cathecart exclaimed, raising his wine glass. "To a wonderful meal and Christmas Day!"

"To Christmas!"

Bobbi touched her glass to his, then they repeated the gesture with their two children, carefully, so they wouldn't spill their cranberry juice on her good white tablecloth.

The remains of a marvelous Christmas dinner were spread before them—turkey with all the trimmings—and a centerpiece of holly interwoven with fresh pine boughs. Bayberry candles in silver holders cast a flickering glow upon their happy faces. But there was a different kind of glow around them as well, that of a loving family spending precious time together. They had much to be thankful for, and their appreciation was quite visible in their sparkling eyes.

"Can I go play with my train set now?" seven-year-old David Jr. asked.

"Not yet, Davey. You haven't finished your peas."

"I hate peas! They look like fish eyeballs."

His little sister made a gagging sound. "Gross, Davey!"

"Yeah, eyeballs!" He picked one up off his plate and held it in front of little Tessa's face. "See! It's looking at you. You eat 'em and the fish can look around inside you!"

"Mommy! Make him stop!"

"That'll be quite enough of that, young man," his father ordered sternly. "Or no pumpkin pie later."

"Aw, Dad!"

Bobbi was comforting five-year-old Tessa, who had eaten all her peas like a good girl but was now seriously considering puking them back up. "They're a vegetable, sweetie. That's all. And ever so good for you. Watch." She put a forkful into her own mouth and chewed, patting her stomach. "Mmm!"

Tessa wasn't entirely convinced, but at least she was no longer as green as the peas. She stuck her tongue out at her brother when Bobbi's back was turned, then a mischievous grin turned up the corners of her tiny mouth.

"Can I play with Davey's trains too?" she asked.

"No!" Davey yelled. "That's man stuff!"

"A girl can be just as good a driver as a boy!"

"Children!" Bobbi shook her finger at them. "No more yelling. Both of you may leave the table now. And I'd better hear nothing but happy, cooperative voices in that living room."

"But, Mom!"

"Let your sister run the trains, Davey. It won't kill you to share them for a little while."

"Aw, gee."

He got off his chair and slunk into the living room, hanging his head. Tessa skipped after him. "I swear," Bobbi said with a sigh. "Sometimes I think those two sit around plotting things that'll drive me crazy. Eyeballs!"

"Well, they do sort of look like them, don't you think?" her husband asked, pushing the remaining peas on his plate around with his fork. "Boy! Am I stuffed!"

"Not you too!"

David got up and came to stand behind her chair, leaning over and putting his arms around her. "I'm teasing! It was a wonderful meal, honey. Perfect. Just like you."

"I'll bet you say that to all the girls."

"Are you kidding? I can barely keep up with you; what use would I have for another woman?"

Bobbi stood up and hugged him. "See to it that you don't think of anything, buster." They kissed. "I want to go play with my new toys too," she told him, eyes agleam.

"Ssh! Don't let the kids hear you. They'll want to see, and if Davey thinks peas look like eyeballs, just imagine what he'd come up with for a twelve-inch vibrator."

She slipped her hands down his back and squeezed his buns. "I want to see what *you* can come up with, lover boy."

"Bobbi! The children!"

"They're playing." She cocked her head, frowning. "A bit too quietly for my taste. We'd better look."

The pair went to the living room doorway and peeked in on their children. Davey was explaining the finer points of train operation to his sister. She was listening, eyes full of wonder and a certain sisterly adoration.

"They do love one another, don't they?"

David nodded. "Sure. Just as much as we love them."

"And each other." Bobbi put her arm around his waist. "I'm so lucky to have all of you."

"It just gets better and better, doesn't it?"

"You said it. I'm so happy! Thank you!"

He smiled at her. "For?"

"Everything!" she exclaimed. "For marrying me. For giving me two beautiful children." Bobbi leaned close, whispering in his ear. "And for being a slave to my every desire. I can't wait till they're in bed!"

"Neither can I. Come on, I'll help you clean up, then we can relax and watch them wear themselves out."

They started carrying plates into the kitchen, stacking them near the sink. With the Christmas bonus she'd gotten from Carol this year, Bobbi planned to buy a dishwasher at long last. But there was something kind of cozy about standing hip to hip with David, doing them by hand.

"I wish . . ."

"What do you wish?" he asked her.

"I can't help thinking about poor Carol."

David laughed. "Poor Carol is doing pretty well for herself. Thank heaven. With your salary we're finally able to afford some luxuries."

"I'm not talking about financially," Bobbi said. "It's the rest of her life that's a mess. I can tell she wants kids by the way she acts around Davey and Tessa. But if she keeps running away from commitment like she does, she'll never have any. I wish she wasn't so afraid of love."

"You can't blame her. From what I know of her past, that particular emotion hasn't been kind to her."

"I can so blame her!" his wife objected. "Okay, so Frank treated her like his own personal gold mine, but that was years ago. She can't go on like this! If she doesn't change, Carol Applegate will end up a sour old maid. You mark my words!"

Tick. Tock. Tick. Tock.

30

Four generations of O'Phealans packed The Naked Waitress to the rafters, chattering, shouting, and dancing a wild Irish reel to the sound or raucous music. They had their own built-in band, with two fiddle players, three guitarists, and Uncle John on bass, plus a couple of tin whistle tooters for good measure.

And there were plenty left to enjoy the show, well over fifty all told, from ninety-five-year-old Grandma O'Phaelan to six-month-old Jesse, whose last name was actually Smith but was considered part of the brood nonetheless. The din was unbelievable, and the body heat alone was sufficient to warm the pub even without the pot-bellied stove.

It could get confusing. A shout for Pat would bring six men on the run. There were plenty of Marys, quite a few Mikes, and a fair number of Seans as well. All of the latter were having as good a time as anyone else, save one.

The Sean Patrick O'Phaelan who would have to completely restock his bar after this bash wasn't enjoying himself at all.

Not that he begrudged them a drop. In fact,

he'd had a dram or two himself. But it wasn't lifting his spirits any, because even surrounded by all these people, he was still painfully aware of the one person missing.

A tall, muscular man with green eyes and auburn hair going silver approached him. "Sean!"

"What?"

"Aye!"

"Over here!"

"Away with the lot of you!" the man exclaimed. "I'm talking to this sorry lout with his nose in a glass and his chin on the tops of his shoes. What's wrong with you, lad? Santa put coal in your stocking?"

Sean looked at his father and managed a small smile. "You might say that," he replied. "Carol gave me a Christmas present. The boot."

"Well." The elder O'Phaelan took a seat beside his son and put his arm around his shoulder. "I'm sorry to hear that. I liked that girl; so did your mother. She was hoping to hear the pitter-patter of a new generation of little O'Phaelans in our house soon. I don't suppose there's a chance—"

"None. If someone tells you to get lost often enough, eventually you take the hint."

"Ah. It's a tough old world, son. But it's a big one too. Have your wake for a lost love and then dance a jig with a new one," his father told him sagely. "The best cure for a broken heart is to get it next to another one as soon as you can."

With that he winked, gave Sean a hearty slap on the back, and went to do some more dancing.

"Where have I heard that before?" Sean muttered.

"From me."

Sean spun around on his stool to find Maureen gazing at him. She was looking particularly saucy, her face flushed from having taken a spin around the floor with almost every man there. Right now she had her eyes set on Sean and a very determined look on her face.

"I told you she'd make a fool of you," Maureen said.

"I'm not particularly in the mood to be reminded of that just now, Maureen."

"Tough." She sat down beside him. "Look, Sean. We're not getting any younger, you and I. I've been a wild one in my day, but so have you. Now we're both looking to settle. You could do worse," she said, pressing herself against him.

"Maureen . . ."

She got to her feet again and took his hand. "Dance with me. Come on. It's Christmas!"

"I told you, I'm not in the mood."

"Hey!" Maureen bellowed at the band. "Play something sad and sweet for your brokenhearted relative and me! He's in need of some comfort."

"And you're certainly built for that, Maureen!" some wag in the crowd bellowed back.

But the band was happy to oblige. Under the focus of all those eyes, Sean had little choice. He allowed Maureen to lead him into the middle of the room, where they joined a dozen other couples who were ready for a slow one. If ever there was a sadder sound than a fiddle playing a slow Celtic ballad, Sean had never heard it.

Then one of his sisters started singing. It was a story of ill-fated lovers dying an ocean apart, and her voice was so sweet that he felt tears sting his eyes. And there was Maureen, cheeks wet with her own tears, looking at him and offering him everything, including her heart.

Sean lowered his head to kiss her ruby red lips.

Tick. Tock. "Stop!"

Carol tried to claw her way up through an ocean of fuzzy confusion, but couldn't seem to open her eyes. She settled for yelling at the top of her lungs. "No! This is my goddamn dream, and I'm not going to let it happen!"

Suddenly she found herself in the pub, grabbing Sean's hand and wrenching it from Maureen's grasp. The crowd parted to let them through. But Carol noticed their faces were becoming blurry and each step was like moving through molasses. Then everything disappeared, to be replaced by a foggy veil of white. She still held Sean's hand. They were in bed together, her bed, surrounded by billowing clouds.

"What the hell?" she muttered.

"Isn't this what you wanted?"

Carol looked at him, realizing he was no longer dressed like the Ex of Xmas present. In fact he wasn't dressed at all. "No! I mean . . . what the hell is going on?"

He shrugged. "Like you said, it's your dream."

It didn't feel like a dream. She reached out to touch his chest. Warm, solid, definitely real. Then again, her mind seemed filled with the same vapor that swirled around them and no longer capable of recognizing reality.

But she did recognize the naked form stretched out beside her. Her gaze roved over the planes and angles of Sean's body, remembering every muscle as only a trained artist could. Unable to help herself, Carol traced every curve with her hand.

His manhood stirred at her touch. She gasped, eyes gleaming wickedly. "A dream?"

"Does it really matter?" Sean asked, starting to pull her nightgown up on her legs.

For a figment of her imagination, he was very persuasive. Sean's fingertips glided along the warm, smooth skin of her inner thigh, teasing, coaxing, awakening still more sweet memories in her already tingling nerve endings.

A dream, a hoax, she couldn't tell and she didn't care. "No," Carol said softly, "it doesn't matter at all." She pulled her nightgown over her head and settled back down beside him, reveling in the feel of his body against hers.

Sean didn't speak of love. He didn't need to. His gentle touch upon her breasts said everything, all his feelings for her and the way he cherished her. Carol's body replied in kind, without confusion or hesitation. Her nipples hardened beneath his hand, inviting him to taste. She moaned at the tender teasing of his lips and tongue, then her blue eyes beckoned to him, communicating a demand for a taste of her own. They kissed, deeply, tongues dueling in the secret caverns of their open mouths, their only language that of heartfelt sighs.

Nipping at his chest, her hand caressing the taut muscles of his stomach, Carol felt him come fully alive. Her gladiator was preparing for a sensuous battle. But the statue she had created was only cold stone; Sean was warm, his heart beating beneath her lips, a pulse that was echoed by his manhood. He throbbed against her stomach, calling out to her in a silent, erotic voice that asked for immediate attention. She obliged, taking him in both hands, feeling his heat on the tip of her tongue as she slowly drew as much of him into her mouth as she dared.

He groaned in ecstasy, but needed more. Her sensual dreams of earlier had made her ready and willing to provide. Carol rolled to her back, wrapping her long, lithe legs around his hips. Sean entered her inch by inch, his mind reeling at her desperate need. She tossed her head from side to side in joyful abandon, giving herself totally to him and the pleasure flooding through her.

Gasping for breath, Carol reached out for him and pulled him fully atop her, relishing his weight, moaning in satisfaction as she felt the final delicious inches of his masculinity slip inside her. He was still for a moment, kissing her lips, her face, her throat; and then Sean began an easy, gentle rhythm.

Carol clutched at his hard buttocks, urging him to increase his pace. She wanted all of him, as much as she could stand and more. Passion clouded her mind now, blocking out all other thoughts. Arching her back, meeting his every movement and thrust, she caressed his sides, his chest, then took his head in her hands and demanded to be kissed. His tongue filled her mouth, as his manhood filled her completely again and again, making her heart race and turning her every breath into a moan of desire.

At long last she cried out, clutching at his back as her orgasm washed over her in wave after wave. Sean tumbled after, his own hoarse cries mingling with Carol's, sweet music to both their ears. When their shuddering pleasure finally came to an end, they rolled to their sides, still joined, sharing the simple joy of being entwined in each other's arms. Their bodies were slick with perspiration, overheated from their passionate efforts.

Slowly he withdrew from her. Carol smiled at him, caressing his strong chin with her fingertips. "Now that's what I call being grabbed by the Christmas spirit!"

Sean's expression remained serious. "I have one more thing to show you before I leave."

"Leave? I don't want you to leave!"

"That's up to you, Carol. It always has been."

He held something up in front of her face. Carol focused on it. "A ring?"

"A wedding ring."

Her face was flushed, but now she felt all the blood drain away. There was love in her heart. The things she had been somehow magically shown tonight had moved her. But she was still afraid.

"I . . . I can't."

Sean nodded sadly. "You've been reminded of how beautiful love can be, shown the joy it can bring. And still you're frightened of embracing it to the fullest?"

"Yes." She turned away, on the verge of tears. "Don't you understand? I've felt the pain of love too, Sean. And I can't risk going through it again."

"The past is gone; the best we can do is learn from it. Our futures will always be an uncertainty. But the present," he told her, "the present we can hold in our hands, shape it to our own designs." He held the ring out to her. "Seize the moment before it's gone, Carol."

She buried her face in a pillow, sobbing. "I can't!"

"Then you have no choice but to allow the present to shape you," Sean told her. "And suffer the consequences."

Tick. Tock. Tick. Tock.

31

Carol didn't know how long she'd been asleep. But her pillow was still wet with bitter tears, so it couldn't have been more than a few minutes. She was cold. The least the Ex of Xmas present could have done for her was spirit her back into her nightgown.

As she slipped into it, a thought occurred to her. "Wait a damn minute!" she muttered angrily. "Why are the sheets all tangled?" She smoothed them with her hands. "They're damp too! All right, Sean! I'm onto your little game. The jig is up!" Carol grabbed a handful of the bedcurtains, jerking them wide open.

And was confronted by a most terrible apparition. It was dressed in a black robe, its face concealed by the folds of a deep hood. Its hands, if it had hands, were likewise hidden in the robe's sleeves.

"Frank?" Silence. "Sean?" More silence.

It couldn't be Richard in there. For one thing he probably wouldn't even be able to move until sunup. For another, he was still under the impression she was ready to succumb to his charms.

"You are the Ex of Xmas yet to come?" she asked.

The figure slowly nodded. That cinched it. Richard had no idea she was planning to dump him and wouldn't dump easily in any case.

"Okay, Sean. Or Frank. No more bullshit! On the count of three, you either take off that silly get-up and apologize or I'll—"

The Ex of Xmas yet to come held out a hand, the slender, skeletal fingers rattling just inches from her nose. Carol was a strong-willed, tough-minded woman; it took more than a skeleton to frighten her. But on the little finger of that bony hand was a ring, a ring exactly like the one she wore even now on her own pinkie, a graduation gift from her father.

This was supposed to be her! The Ex of Xmas yet to come wasn't a future lover, it was the ex–Carol Applegate! She gasped and fell back onto the bed, out like a light.

Tick. Tock. Tick. Tock.

32

Carol opened her eyes and looked around, shivering. At first she thought the spirit's spell had gone awry, because she felt completely awake and aware. Then she realized that the scene before her was even more dreamlike than any of the others, as if it hadn't come into full focus yet.

Of course. The future. She peered through the haze and finally realized precisely where she was. But she didn't move from her shadowy corner, somehow knowing that she wasn't really there at all.

Sean stood at the window of his apartment above The Naked Waitress, looking out at the snow coming down outside. Another annual O'Phaelan Christmas party was in full tilt downstairs. Happy voices and thumping music filled the old building, vibrating the floor. He was smiling, but it was a wistful smile, that of a man in deep contemplation.

There was a gleeful shriek behind him. He turned as a little girl dashed into the room, black pigtails flying.

"Daddy!" she cried. "Save me!"

"Here now! What's all this?"

"Granpa's gonna eat me!"

She ran over to him and hid behind one of his legs, peering past his knee at the doorway. A big man with silver hair appeared, his arms outstretched.

"I want my supper!" he bellowed.

"Your supper?" Sean asked, his eyes twinkling. "I don't have your supper. What did it look like?"

His father stomped around the room, pretending to search. "Three feet tall it was, barely a mouthful, but young and juicy in the bargain!"

The little girl clutched Sean's legs, giggling. He leaned nonchalantly against the window sill. "Three feet tall, eh? Young and juicy, you say? That does sound mighty tasty, but I'm afraid I haven't seen it. Do you suppose it's hiding in the closet?"

He opened the closet door. "No!"

"Under the couch?"

"No!" he roared, then looked right at her. "There it is!"

Sean's daughter shrieked and pulled on his pant leg, demanding to be picked up. He did so, swinging her around in the air. "This? Why, this can't be your supper! It's too cute to eat!"

"Well, I suppose you're right. Just a taste, then."

While Sean held her, his father took one of her arms and nibbled on it, making her laugh hysterically. He made a face. "Ach! Too sweet."

"Granpa's silly!" she exclaimed, yanking her arm away from him and hugging Sean's neck.

"Yes, he is, isn't he?" He sat down on the couch, placing her on his knee and bouncing his leg up and down. She squealed happily, her little hand wrapped around two of his fingers for balance. "Ho! Ride 'em, cowgirl!"

"Stop, Daddy! I gotta go tinkle!"

Sean stopped bouncing her and set her gently on her feet, giving her a pat on the bottom. "Need help?"

"I want Mommy."

"Go get her, then. She's in the bedroom."

The little girl skipped off. Sean's father sat down beside him with a sigh. "Quite a handful, that one."

"Yes indeed. And another on the way. You tell that crew of yours to get a move on with our new house, hear?"

"Final inspection's next Wednesday. Soon enough?"

Sean laughed. "Who knows? Ask the lady to wait."

"Not me. The two of you have been waiting long enough for a second babe as it is." He studied Sean's face. "What's that frown for?"

"Just thinking," he replied with a shrug. "It's the time of year, you know. I can't help it."

His father put a hand on his shoulder. "You have to let her go, son. You have your own life to lead."

"I know. And I'm happy."

He smiled as his young daughter came back

into the living room, followed by his wife, who was very heavy with child. She was smiling too, smugly self-satisfied.

"Come on!" Maureen exclaimed. "Let's us O'Phaelans go down and join the party!"

Watching all this from her shadow-filled corner of the room, Carol began to cry. No one comforted her. "Enough!" She sobbed. "What of *my* future?"

The haze closed in again, then cleared, and she was suddenly in a familiar place. Her own front yard. But something was very wrong.

There was no more two-story Victorian house, no studio, nothing. Just a burned-out hulk sitting forlorn and grim beneath a blanket of snow, with only a charred remnant of a wall here and there to give a clue that a cozy, much-loved home had once stood on this spot.

Carol wanted to ask what was going on. She could feel a presence, as if someone was watching over her, but could see no one. Then she heard voices. Three people emerged from the trees lining the driveway. One of them was a local real estate agent, the other a young couple Carol didn't know. The woman asked the question for her.

"What on earth happened?"

"A fire," the real estate agent replied. "The former owner was an artist, a sculptor, with a studio right there." He pointed to where the converted garage had been. "There were a lot of flammable things around. Wood chips, oily finishing rags, things like that. Spontaneous combustion, the fire department said. Terrible thing. And the day after Christmas too."

Carol put her hands on her hips and yelled at them. "I beg your pardon! I'm always careful! The place is as neat as can be and all my rags go into a fire-safe container filled with water!"

The three people walked past her, oblivious. "Well, it's a nice piece of land," the young man said, "but I don't think I'd ever be comfortable here."

"Never," the woman agreed. "Show us something else."

They strolled on down her driveway, disappearing over the hill. Carol was alone again, beside herself with rage. "No! I demand to go back to the day this happened. Show me!"

Again the haze closed in. She heard ticking. But it was a different kind of ticking than before. This was soft, almost inaudible, a steady electronic kind of noise. As the haze cleared, she saw Richard's face hovering over her.

"What's that?" he asked. "Oh, would you like me to show you how it works?" Richard smiled. "Why, certainly, dear. I'm sure you'll find it interesting. Not very useful, I'm afraid, but interesting."

Carol looked around wildly. They were in her studio. The blinds were drawn. Richard was standing at the workbench, some strange device in his hand. She was *on* the bench. There was a gag around her mouth and her hands and feet were tied to the bench with soft cotton rope.

And all she was wearing was a frilly teddy, one so blatantly risque she would never have bought it, let alone put it on. Judging by her embarrassing predicament, she reasoned that the lingerie was Richard's Christmas present to her, and that she hadn't gotten into it by choice.

As horrible as that realization was, an even greater horror dawned when she figured out that the ticking sound was coming from the device Richard held in his elegant, graceful hands. A bomb!

She tried to talk. "Mmph! Mmhmhm!"

"Patience, little one! I went through hell to procure this device; I don't intend to rush the installation." He ran a fingertip down her bare leg, grinning as she writhed and jerked her head from side to side. "It was nice of you to get rid of O'Phaelan so we could be alone at last. Don't worry. I'll be done in a moment, and then we can enjoy each other to the fullest."

"Hmmhmm!" Carol objected, looking at the bomb.

He chuckled. "Relax! Owing to the wonder of modern technology, it's perfectly safe until activated by remote control. I could beat on it with a hammer if I wished."

Richard moved away from her, going to his sculpture. He carefully tipped it onto its side and began inserting the bomb into the sculpture's conveniently hollow base. As he worked, he explained what he was doing, his voice cheerful.

"It's really quite simple. A bit of plastic explosive, a detonator, and a timing device. And of course my design for the base. This hollow in the heavy bronze acts to shape the charge, forcing the explosion downward. A wall of flame and expanding gases will spew forth, spreading to an area approximately twelve feet in diameter in less than a second, propelling everything in its path toward the target below. The devastation will be total, enough to flatten an entire room and anyone unfortunate enough to get in the way. And I assure you, there will indeed be someone in that position when I set it off."

Carol pulled frantically at her bonds. But it was no use; as with everything else Richard did, the knots he had tied were expert. She was completely at his mercy. He heard her struggling and glanced at her.

"You see, Carol, I'm afraid I told you a little fib. This isn't for the American Ski Team at all. It's to be donated—anonymously, of course—to the art-loving chairman of the Sheti Mining Corporation, who as you may know has a home nearby. He also has a little gallery all his own, right above his bedroom."

"Hyy!"

"Why? Simple. He's in my way. The rest of the board will be lost without him, and while they're fighting, I'll be quietly finishing the job I came to Tithe for in the first place; taking control of their company."

Richard finished his installation by packing some of Carol's modeling clay into the base and smoothing it off. Satisfied, he came back to her side. "There now. All done. Let me remove this so we can chat for a bit."

Carol briefly considered yelling for help, then realized how absurd it would be. They were obviously alone, a result of her finally sending Sean away. And her house wasn't near enough to anything else for her screams to be heard.

Besides, she had already seen what was going to happen. Now she was taking a peek backward to find out why. The Ex of Xmas present had given her a chance to avert this particular future and she had refused. Was what Sean said true? Was she now doomed to suffer the consequences of her decision?

"This is crazy, Richard! You'll get caught!"

He laughed. "No, I don't think so. No one will know it was I who gave him the statue."

"But they'll trace it back to me," she pointed out.

"There won't be enough left of it to identify, and besides, I made sure it's unlike anything you've ever done before, remember? I've also taken the liberty of removing your signature," Richard informed her. "Sorry. There goes your chance at immortality."

"Other people know I was working on a project for you!"

He clucked his tongue sorrowfully. "You're not dealing with an amateur, Carol. When it comes to making intricate, foolproof plans, I'm a genius. Yes, other people know you made this ugly thing—it should be some comfort to know it suits the chairman's tastes to a T, by the way—but they'll assume it was destroyed in the fire I am going to start in a little while. And you," Richard added with a particularly nasty smile, "will mysteriously disappear, just an eccentric artist prone to making unusual holiday changes who decided to take off for parts unknown."

Carol gasped. "No!"

"Face it, Carol. You're a victim of fate. I made a careful study of the artists in this area before I came. The type of work you produced was perfect for my purposes, but I also needed someone who was unattached, easy to get next to. And there you were, on the verge of a break-up with O'Phaelan, ripe for my attentions."

"That's your undoing!" she cried out. "You can't get rid of me; they'll know we were together today!"

"True. But given your past, people will think you tossed me out on my ear for getting too serious, just as you did with O'Phaelan yesterday. In fact, I'll make sure that is precisely what they think, loudly and in public, long before the fire and your absence are even discovered."

Carol was terrified. It was like one of those dreams where she had to run but couldn't make her feet move. Only this wasn't a dream, it was her future, a path she was stuck on because of her fear of commitment, her failure to seize the moment.

"Stop this! Please! I want love! I want Sean and marriage and babies! I want to live!"

No haze descended upon her. The chance

was gone. This was all happening, right now, as real as the wicked gleam she saw in Richard's eyes.

"But of course you'll live, you silly woman! In total luxury I might add, on my own remote and very private island. A prisoner to love! A slave to my every desire!"

Richard ran his hands over her scantily clad form, along the curve of her breasts, down her sides to the soft skin of her inner thighs. Then he dipped his head to nibble on her neck. Carol thrashed desperately.

"Such fire!" Richard exclaimed. "You'll learn to enjoy my touch, Carol. You'll see. I'll be very good to you, give you everything your heart desires. In time, you might even come to love me and want *my* children!" He reached into his coat pocket and pulled out a vial of pills. "Now, be a good girl and take one of these, and before you know it, you'll be in your new home!"

As he started to uncork the vial, Carol started to scream.

33

"Wait! I've had a change of heart!"

Carol sat bolt upright in bed, gasping for breath. Her alarm clock was buzzing loudly on the bedside table. She yanked the bedcurtains aside and slammed her hand on the off button, squinting at the sunlight streaming cheerfully through her bedroom window. The day had dawned bright and clear.

But what day?

There was a noise outside. After jumping out of bed, she dashed to the window and opened it, breathing deeply of the crisp morning air. A young boy pulling a sled loaded with newspapers was trudging down her driveway toward the street, which had been recently plowed, Carol saw. A couple of four-wheel-drive vehicles growled by on their way into town.

"Jimmy!" she called.

He paused and turned to look at her. "Yes'm?"

"Is this Christmas Day?"

"Course it is!" he called back, looking at her with a puzzled expression. "Weird storm, huh? All that snow last night and now look at it!" He waved his hand at the clear blue sky. "Like magic!"

Carol laughed, clapping her hands together. "Yes, Jimmy! Just like magic!"

"Well, see you. I'm going to go play with my new sled as soon as I'm done with my route. Merry Christmas!"

"Merry Christmas!"

Dashing to her closet, Carol grabbed a sweater and a pair of jeans. "Green panties! It's definitely a day for another pair of green panties!" she exclaimed merrily.

After the night she'd had, she should have been dragging, but instead she felt refreshed and well rested. Perhaps the whole crazy thing had been nothing but an intense, incredibly vivid dream after all. It didn't matter. Her panic and confusion were gone. For perhaps the first time since her divorce, she knew exactly what she wanted to do.

She almost fell flat on her face several times in her haste to get dressed. The bedroom door was still locked from the inside, exactly as she'd left it last night, but she didn't have time to puzzle over it. An urgent mission awaited her. Carol unlocked the door and emerged into the hallway.

The house was quiet. That was fine with her; in a few moments all hell would break loose. She went downstairs and opened the door to her studio, not bothering to close it behind her. After grabbing a ten-pound sledge hammer from beneath her workbench, she swung it up to her shoulder and approached Richard's sculpture, grinning from ear to ear.

"One for the money." BANG! "Two for the show." BANG! "Three for the bullshit and out you go!" BANG!

The intricately crisscrossed stainless steel wires were resilient, but no match for the hammer. She swung again and again, beads of perspiration popping out on her forehead with the effort. When the sculpture was little more than a misshapen mass of twisted wires, Carol knocked it off the metal table it was sitting on and started in on the bronze base. This was tougher going but she kept at it, smashing it to bits, oblivious to the noise—and to the bleary-eyed man who came up behind her.

"My statue!" Richard cried.

Puffing and panting, Carol turned around to find him standing in the studio doorway. From the way he looked, he had one hell of a hangover. That made her smile, as did his horrified expression.

"Spoils your little plan, doesn't it?" she asked.

"Have you taken leave of your senses?" He came into the studio and gazed down at the remains of the sculpture, mouth agape. "You've ruined it!"

She stood there with the hammer resting on her shoulder, one arm slung over the handle to balance it there. "You'll just have to find some other way to take over Sheti Mining."

"I don't—"

"Shut up!" Carol interrupted harshly. Eyes

narrowed and teeth clenched, she grasped the handle of the sledge. "I'm onto your foolproof plan now, Palance. There won't be a take-over, or an assassination attempt, and I sure as hell won't be your love slave!" She took a step toward him.

Richard immediately backed up. His face was white, and little wonder. He was confronted with a madwoman, tendrils of hair plastered to her forehead and murder in her eyes.

"You're insane!"

"Maybe I am!" She cackled gleefully, lifting the hammer above her head. "So you'd better get out of here before I split your skull!"

Richard turned and dashed out of the studio, tripping over his own feet as he burst out the front door, Carol right behind him. He hit the driveway running, fell down, picked himself up and continued on, yelling at the top of his lungs. "Help! Save me! She's lost her mind!"

Carol watched him slip and slide down to the end of the driveway, where he stood in the street, waving frantically at a passing truck. Grinning with triumph, she shut the door and turned around. Frank was standing in the living room, looking totally bewildered.

Then he saw the hammer. "Oh, shit! Listen, Carol—"

"Come here, Frank."

He shook his head. "I'd rather not."

After leaning the hammer against the wall, Carol grabbed his coat from a stand near the front door and carried it over to him. Frank watched her warily.

"Here. Put this on," she ordered. He did so. She zipped it up for him, then took his hand and led him toward the door. "Thank you for the things you showed me last night."

"Excuse me?"

"And thank you for the good times," Carol continued. "We really were in love once. It was great while it lasted."

"Yeah. It was." He tried to kiss her. She pushed him away. "Hey! I thought you were saying thank you?"

"Oh, what the hell." Carol kissed him sweetly on his bearded cheek. "That's in remembrance of the love we once shared," she said.

Frank smiled. "As long as you're filled with all this Christmas spirit, could we discuss that loan?"

"And this is for all the rest!" Carol raised her knee swiftly, hitting him solidly in the groin. "You bastard!"

"Oof! Oh!"

"We're divorced, Frank. Kaput. I don't want to see you around here again, not even in a dream!"

She spun him around, opened the door, put a foot on his backside, and propelled him head-first out the door into a snowbank. "Dig your truck out, point it anywhere except Tithe, and get a life! Mine's full up!" Carol yelled, then she closed the door again and locked it.

Sean came down the stairs, yawning sleepily.

He was wearing the pink robe she'd found for Richard. On him it was too small, but rather cute in a cuddly sort of way.

"What the hell's going on down here?" he asked.

"Oh, nothing," Carol replied. "Just exorcising a couple of spirits."

"Huh?"

"Never mind. Sleep well?"

He nodded, smiling. "Like a log. You?"

"I'm not really sure. But I can't complain. There were some interesting highlights," she told him.

"Highlights?" Sean asked, frowning. "What do you mean?"

"Tell you what. You get a fire going while I make us some coffee, and I'll show you exactly what I mean."

Sean shrugged his big shoulders and went to the fireplace. Carol headed for the kitchen, singing a joyful tune. When the coffee was ready she poured them both a cup and returned to the living room. The fire was ablaze. She plugged in her Christmas tree, lit some candles, then joined him on the couch. They sat in silence for a bit, sipping coffee and letting the warmth of the flames and the peace of Christmas soak into them.

Then Carol stood up and slowly started taking off her clothes. Sean arched his eyebrows. "Highlights, huh? You must have had some interesting dreams!"

"I did." When all she had on was her Christmas panties, she lay down on the bear rug in front of the fireplace. It wasn't a real bear skin, but was still marvelously soft on hers. She held her arms out to him. "Come here, Mr. Christmas present, and make them all come true."

Sean got to his feet, hands on his hips. "Make that Mr. Christmas forever and I will."

"Anything you say, love," Carol told him. She reached up and grabbed the end of his terry-cloth belt and pulled, eyes agleam as the robe fell open. "Forever it is."

Discarding the robe, Sean slipped down beside her, taking her in his arms. His touch was tender and gentle, his eyes full of the love he felt for her. Where once this seriousness caused her fear, now Carol felt only joy.

"I have something for you," Sean told her.

Her smile was wicked. "So I see!" Carol took his swelling manhood in her hands. "And I want it all!"

"For someone who looks like a Christmas angel, you sure have the devil in your eyes." He reached under the tree and retrieved a small box from the other presents there, which he handed to her. "First this. Then I'm all yours."

Carol pulled off the gift wrap and opened the box. Inside was a finely wrought gold ring. "It's beautiful!"

"Will you marry me?"

"Yes!" She slipped the ring on her finger, tears in her eyes. "Yes! Can we announce it today, at your family Christmas party?" *In front of Maureen,* she added silently.

"Try and stop me!" he replied. "Now, where were we?"

She took his head in her hands and pulled him down to kiss her. "Right about here will do for a start."

His tongue darted into her mouth, to be met by her own. They drank their fill of one another's sweetness, then moved on, like greedy children who had found everything they asked for beneath the tree on Christmas morning. Sean kissed her breasts, feeling each tip harden beneath his lips. He suckled her, then ran his hands along the smooth skin of her sides, across her stomach, and down her long, beautifully shaped legs, treasuring every inch of her.

Carol treasured him as well, with her eyes and mouth and tongue, while he removed her festive panties, revealing all of her to his hungry gaze. He brushed her pale-blond hair with the tips of his fingers, chuckling throatily as he kissed his way down her inner thigh.

She moaned and stiffened at the first delicate touch of his inquiring tongue, but soon relaxed again, melting with a sigh when he reached his ultimate goal. While Sean spoke to her body in this most intimate language, Carol posed a few questions herself, with her own tongue, and though he sighed, Sean certainly didn't melt. He throbbed, so hot and powerful, that she at last could take no more teasing.

Sean settled himself atop her and Carol took his weight and masculinity without hesitation, urging him deeper inside. They made slow, languorous love in front of the blazing fire, their skin warmed by the flames and the heat of their desire, the twinkling lights on the Christmas tree reflected in their shining eyes.

Finally, in a mutual gasping wave, they plunged into the sweet abyss that only lovers know, clinging to each other for the dear life they would now share together. Maybe the future would always be an uncertainty, but they would go into it in one another's arms, living moment by moment and seizing each one to keep as their own.

As Carol lay in her afterglow, looking up at the Christmas tree, she felt so much love inside her she thought certain her heart couldn't contain it all. Was it possible to be so happy? This was her traditional time of change, but could she really have changed so much in just one night?

Tick. Tock. Tick. Tock.

"No! I'll never let him go again!"

Carol grabbed hold of Sean and held on tight. But he didn't disappear. He kissed her on the tip of the nose and asked, "What's wrong? You look like you've seen a ghost!"

"Do you hear that noise?"

Sean listened. "Like a clock?"

"Oh, my God!" Carol rolled over and got to her knees, listening intently. The ticking was coming from one of the presents beneath the tree. She bent to read the tag. "For the most obliging sculptor I've ever met, from your hot tub companion. May you count the hours we're apart, as do I. Richard!" Carol cried. "That's how he got it into the house! Disguised as a present!"

She jumped to her feet, picking the gaily wrapped package up with trembling hands. "We've got to get rid of this. Now!"

"What the—"

"Don't ask questions!" Carol interrupted hysterically. "Quick! Where can we put it where it won't do any damage?"

"Damage?"

"I saw it in a dream! It's a bomb!"

Sean sighed. "Carol, this isn't . . ." He trailed off, seeing the terror in her eyes. "Okay! Calm down. How about that big metal container in your studio?"

"No! A fire could start in there!"

"How? It's filled with water, isn't it?"

"I mean a fire in the studio. Don't argue!"

He got to his feet, slipping back into the pink robe. "Give it here. I'll put it in the container and then stick the container outside in the snow. How's that?"

"Do it!" she exclaimed, gladly giving him the package.

Carol watched him carefully, making sure he did as promised. He came back into the house, shivering and rubbing his bare feet. She ran into his arms and hugged him, covering his cold face with kisses.

"Thank you! Oh, Sean, I love you so much!"

"I love you too!" He chuckled. "You know something, Carol? You were destined to become an O'Phaelan. With your eccentricities, you'll fit right in."

34

"Ow! Me achin' 'ead!"

Percy groaned as he opened his eyes. Then he opened them even wider. He was in a strange bed in a strange place, nothing really new for him as much as he and his employer moved around. But there was a woman beside him. A very soft, very warm woman. He lifted an edge of the blankets and took a peek. Percy smiled. "Oh yes! Now I remember!"

Maureen stirred, wrapping her arms around his neck. "Good morning, Percy," she mumbled. "It is morning?"

"Indeed! Open your eyes to a beautiful Christmas Day, my pet. It's a wonderful sight!" He kissed her forehead. "And so are you." A frown furrowed his brow for a moment, then he grinned again. "Did we really . . ."

"Did we ever!" Maureen told him, opening her eyes at last. Memories washed over her, every bit as warm as the sunlight streaming through the bedroom window of Sean's apartment. "In the bathtub, on the living-room floor, in the kitchen. Did we get around to the bed?" She wiggled a little, hearing the screech of a broken caster. "Yes, we definitely got around to the bed. I hope Sean won't be too angry with us."

"I shall reimburse him for the damage." Percy cuddled up to her, laying his head atop her ample bosom. "You're quite a woman, Maureen."

She giggled. "I didn't do it by myself, silly. You, Percival Stevens, are one hell of a man!" she assured him, stroking his aristocratic face. "Talk about appearances deceiving! My God!"

"Yes, well, I tried to keep my end up."

"Mmm! And I think it's coming up again right now!"

He smiled, pleased with himself. "Why, so it is!"

"Whoa, big fella! I've got just the sugar you want!"

Maureen rolled on top of him. Her breasts were so large they wrapped all the way around his head. Percy was so large she had to scoot up that far to get him inside of her. Once joined, she pushed herself into a sitting position, grinning down at him wickedly.

He was gasping for breath. "You almost drowned me!" he cried, then pulled her back down. "Do it again!"

"I'll do it again, all right! Hold on to your hat!"

"I don't have a hat."

"Honestly, Percy! You're so literal. Here," she said, taking his hands and placing one on each of her full, jiggling breasts. "Hold on to me instead."

Percy did. Desperately. Maureen started moving atop him, bouncing up and down and grinding her hips in a circle at the same time. The bed squealed for mercy. So did he.

"Oh! My! Don't!" Percy begged.

"Don't?"

He rolled his head from side to side. "Stop!"

"Stop?"

"Don't stop!" Percy grabbed her fulsome buttocks and helped her rock back and forth, lifting his hips to plunge his impressive self completely into her. Now it was Maureen who begged for mercy.

"Geez-us!" she cried. "I've heard of guys not knowing their own strength; you're the first I've met who doesn't know his own length! Easy, Percy, or you really will screw my brains out!"

"Not to worry, dear. I've plenty for both of us."

Percy managed to roll her off of him without dislodging himself, then grabbed her ankles and put one on either side of his head. He plunged into her to the hilt. Maureen's eyes went wide and she moaned.

"Did I hurt you?" he asked, settling himself atop her.

"Hell, no!" Maureen wrapped her arms around him, smothering him against her breasts. "I think I'm in love!"

35

Jack was having a wonderful dream. He was a young man again, and he was with this woman he used to keep time with up in Cripple Creek. She had many fine attributes, among them a good head for business, but it was another type of head he was dreaming about. The woman had the most talented tongue. And right now she was sticking it in his ear, so warm and tantalizing, a prelude to other things.

"Oh, darlin'!" he murmured.

"Heeaw!" Betsy brayed.

He came fully awake, pushing her muzzle away from his ear. His face was all wet. "Bleah! No offense, Betsy m'love, but you've got a terrible case of morning breath!"

Getting to his feet, Jack took hold of her halter and urged her up as well. He'd been forced into the shed late last night, and though the hay-covered floor had been warm, he still resented having been driven out by Maureen and Percy.

"I don't much like waking up with a mule tongue in my ear, old girl," he told her, "but it's a hell of a lot better than trying to sleep through all that caterwauling! Come to think of it, maybe I'd better go check on 'em, see if they're both all right!"

He gave her some oats, then shoved the shed door open, blinking at the bright sunlight. "Would you look at that!" he exclaimed to the blue sky. "Good morning to you too, Christmas!"

Not much more snow had fallen since he'd made his way out to the shed in the wee hours of the morning, but it was still a hard slog to the back of the pub. He hadn't bothered locking the rear doors; any thief who had enough gumption to ply his trade in a blizzard was welcome to the booty in Jack's opinion. But the place was just as he'd left it. A trifle colder, perhaps. He went to the pot-bellied stove and stoked up the fire.

"Coffee," he muttered. "Then I'll go roust those two sex maniacs before the O'Phaelan brood arrives for the party."

Squeak! Squeak! Squeak!

"Shit! They're already up!" He shook his fist at the ceiling and yelled, "Damn it! Be quick about it! Sean's family'll be here soon!"

Squeakasqueakasqueakasqueak!

Shaking his head, Jack went into the kitchen to make some coffee. While he was banging around, a tall, muscular man with auburn hair going silver tapped on the front door. When he didn't get an answer, he put his key in the lock and opened it, holding it for the slender brunette with him and then stepping inside himself.

"Where is that boy? Sean!"

Jack poked his head out of the kitchen. "Why, Mr. and Mrs. O'Phaelan! You're out early!"

"The advance guard," Sean's father said. He came over and shook the other man's hand. "How have you been, Jack? I don't think I've seen you since the last Christmas party!"

"Oh, keeping busy. How's the construction business?"

Mike O'Phaelan laughed. "That's why I haven't been around. You're still trying to make that hole in the ground up there pay, I suppose?"

While they were talking, Margret O'Phaelan decided to slip up and give her son a Christmas surprise. Jack didn't notice she was missing until he heard the apartment door open.

He whirled around and yelled, "Wait! Sean isn't home!"

"Merry Christmas!" Margret exclaimed as she opened the apartment door. Then she screamed and came running back down the stairs. "Mike! There's some strange man up there walking around in his birthday suit!"

"Is there now?"

She nodded. "And he has an enormous—" Margret clapped a hand over her mouth.

"Oh! So you took a good look, did you?"

"Michael Patrick O'Phaelan!" Her face turned red. "I'll box your ears!"

"That's Percy," Jack explained. "Sean spent

the night at Carol's, you see, and . . . It's a bit complicated. Maureen's up there too."

Sean's father grinned. "Well, what's good for the goose goes for the gander, I always say." He rubbed his hands together, green eyes gleaming. "I'll just nip up and get myself a Christmas eyeful as well!"

"In a pig's eye!" his wife cried. "You'll stay right here and start bringing in the goodies for our party."

He saluted her. "Aye, Captain Margret!" he exclaimed, then he turned toward the door. "Your very wish is my command." When he was a safe distance away, he added, "As long as I get to swab your decks later, that is!"

Margret's face turned even redder. "Get to work! And you!" She pointed at Jack. "You go get that boy of mine and tell him we need help. There'll be fifty hungry, thirsty people here by noon."

Jack saluted her too. "What he said goes for me, ma'am!"

"I beg your pardon!"

"Except for swabbing!" Jack blurted. "My swab barely works anymore! And besides, I might not even remember how!"

"Out!" she bellowed. He dashed for the door. "And somewhere between now and the party, Jack Bensen, take a bath! You smell like a mule!"

36

The knocking on Carol's door was steady and insistent. Reluctantly she pulled herself out of Sean's arms and stood up. They had eaten breakfast and dressed in preparation for the Christmas party, but hadn't made much progress since then.

The first delay was her father's traditional Christmas-morning phone call; Tom Applegate was ecstatic over Carol's news. And her mother had done something that Carol considered a good omen. She didn't sob. Instead she let out a joyous yell that had probably rocked the entire Hawaiian island chain.

Then Carol called her Uncle Fred. He *had* cried, but only out of fond remembrance when she told him she'd found the perfect prince to share her mountain kingdom with at last.

They had intended to head for the pub after that, but the fire was still burning and her living room was so cozy that they had snuggled up again, gazing into the flames.

"I told you not to dig a path. Now they've found us."

"Who?"

"The world."

"Madam, today is the day I plan to tell the whole world I'm going to marry you," Sean said. "Or at least I'm going to tell my family, and that's practically the same thing. So let 'em come!"

Carol went to the door and opened it. Jack practically fell in. "Hello there! Merry Christmas!"

"The same to you, Jack.," Carol said, ushering him inside. She crinkled her nose. "What's that smell?"

"Never mind that! Sean, your mother is at the pub already and in high color. You'd better come help before she runs your father ragged."

He stood up, laughing. "I guess you're right."

Jack watched as Carol and he embraced. "Say, it looks as if things are back to normal around here!"

"As normal as they get," Carol agreed. "We'll be along in a bit, Jack. And by the way . . ."

"I know. Take a shower. Just as soon as Percy and Maureen get out of Sean's apartment—" He stopped, eyes wide. "Oops! Let the cat out of the bag."

"They stayed in my bed last night?" Sean asked.

"Well," Jack said, "from the way things sounded, I'd say they stayed just about everywhere, for a few minutes at a time, anyway. We were all snowed in there last night."

"I see. Where did you sleep?"

"In front of the stove, keeping the home fires

burning," Jack replied. "Until the screaming got too much for me, then I went out to the shed and slept with Betsy. That's why I need a bath and a change of clothes."

Carol was puzzled. "Screaming?"

"Maureen has a tendency to get carried away," Jack said.

"Vocal in love, shall we say?" Sean agreed.

"And just how would you know?" Carol demanded.

He wrapped his arms around her. "Purely secondhand rumor, my love. Honest."

"Uh-huh."

"Hurry and get your coat," Sean told her, releasing her from his embrace. "We have a party to get to, and my mother does not like to be kept waiting."

"I want to wrap up some cookies for your folks, first," she said. "Won't be a sec."

On her way to the kitchen she paused, then turned around and came back. "Jack, what's your opinion of Percy?"

"He's a bit stuffy until you get a few into him," Jack replied, "but then he's a fine boy. Maybe a bit oversexed. But then, so's Maureen. I like him. A damn sight better than his boss, I might add. Why?"

She shook her head and sighed. "I don't know. Just wondering. Maybe he isn't part of the plan."

"Plan?" Jack asked.

"Never mind."

Carol went into the kitchen. Winking, Jack

sidled up to Sean and said, "I don't know how you did it, but it looks to me as if congratulations are in order. By the by, did you know there are snowmobile tracks out in Carol's front yard?"

"Do tell? I guess Santa went high-tech this year."

Jack frowned. "Sure. Oh, I wanted to tell you. Percy let some information slip about Palance's business last night. Seems he's here to take over a mining company of some sort. He wouldn't tell me the name, but I'll bet if we pour some more ale down him today he might—"

"Sheti. The Sheti Mining Corporation."

"You knew?"

Sean nodded. "The chairman of the board is a friend of mine. About a week ago he told me he thought there was someone making a play behind the scenes. I figured it was Palance."

Something fell in the kitchen. "Damn! Sean, could you come help me? This plastic wrap is driving me bonkers!"

"Sure, honey." Sean turned to his friend. "Go tell my mother we'll be there in a bit, Jack. Oh, and tell her I've got a surprise for her too," he added, grinning broadly. "Nothing else, just a surprise. Got that?"

"A surprise? You mean?" Jack whooped. "Yahoo! This is going to be the best party ever!"

He took off, slamming the door behind him in his hurry to be the bearer of good tidings. On his way down the path Sean had shoveled along the side of Carol's house, however, he paused. If there was one thing Jack couldn't pass up, it was an opportunity to snoop. And a big can marked FLAMMABLE sitting in a snowbank seemed like just such an opportunity. He lifted the lid and peered inside.

"What do we have here?"

Jack reached in and pulled out a drenched, gift-wrapped box that floated among the oil-soaked rags. He knew why Carol immersed the rags in water; to prevent spontaneous combustion.

But why a Christmas present?

Aware that Carol and Sean would be along any minute, he carried the dripping package down the driveway and hid behind a big tree to open it. It was a bit of a job, as slick and soggy as it was. He dropped it a couple of times in the process, but finally he got the colored paper off and lifted the lid. Yet another puzzle.

"Now why on earth would anybody want to ruin a perfectly good handmade cuckoo clock?" Jack muttered. He shrugged, tucked it under his arm, and went on his way. Maybe he could fix it. "Crying shame. Cost somebody a bundle, I'll bet."

37

"We really should have stayed and helped out. I mean, after what we did to Sean's bed and all."

Percy shrugged. "I did offer, Maureen. But Mrs. O'Phaelan didn't seem comfortable in my presence."

"Well, you did flash her."

"Pardon?"

"Exposed yourself," Maureen explained.

"I didn't do it on purpose! My trousers were in the bathroom and I was simply going to retrieve them when she burst through the door. Is it my fault she's of a delicate disposition?"

"Margret is hardly delicate, Percy," she informed him, grinning. "It was your, um, statistics that alarmed her. Can't say that I blame her. I nearly fainted at first sight myself." Maureen hugged him. "Are you sure this is okay?"

"Certainly. Mr. Palance was in Denver when the storm hit. I'm sure he's on his way by now, but we'll have plenty of time for a nice, bubbly Christmas bath together before he returns." He opened the door to Richard's condo and waved her in ahead of him. "Besides, he ordered me to have fun, and his unit has the spa."

"Does he have any food?" she asked. "I'm starved!"

"As am I. Why don't you go slip into the tub while I prepare us a bit of breakfast? It's on the second level at the end of the hall."

"Okay." As she climbed the stairs, Maureen started to remove her clothes, draping them on the banister as she went. "But don't be long, will you?"

Percy watched her slow striptease, trembling with excitement. As soon as she disappeared, he made a mad dash for the kitchen. Laughing, Maureen continued on down the hall to Richard's bedroom, then stepped into the master bath. She gasped.

The whirlpool was occupied. Richard Palance was submerged up to his shoulders, his back to the glass door and his head resting on the padded edge of the tub. His eyes were closed.

Maureen debated for a moment, then grinned wickedly and tiptoed to the door of the spa enclosure and opened it, trying to get a better look. "Mr. Palance?" she whispered.

He didn't move. She crept closer, bending over him to peer through the clear, placid water at his naked form. Her grin broadened. Not bad. But no comparison to Percy.

"Ha!" Maureen exclaimed softly. "And you call yourself the boss?"

Percy stepped into the bathroom, nude, bearing a platter of hastily chopped fruit. His eyes focused on Maureen's lovely backside. "Oh, my! Here, let me flip this switch."

The water bubbled to life. Richard's eyes popped open and he lifted his head, thus burying his face in Maureen's dangling breasts.

"Oh, God! I'm blind!"

Maureen jumped back. Richard slipped off the fiberglass bench and sank beneath the bubbling water, thrashing wildly. At last he found his footing and stood up, spluttering for breath. "What do you think you're doing, you great cow!"

"Cow!" Maureen cried, putting her fists on her broad hips. "You watch your mouth, needle dick!"

Percy put the platter of fruit down and entered the enclosure. "I can explain, sir," he said in a businesslike tone, oblivious to the fact he didn't have any clothes on.

"Stevens!" Richard glared at him, grabbing a towel and wrapping it around his waist as he climbed out of the tub. "What's the meaning of this? Why are you and a this . . . this trollop in my bathroom?"

Percy bristled. "Keep a civil tongue in your head, sir! You're talking about the woman I intend to marry!"

"Marry!" Maureen wrapped her arms around him. "Oh, Percy! I accept!"

"This is absurd!" Richard bellowed. "Has the entire town gone insane? Carol Applegate threatens to split my skull; no one would give me a ride so I had to walk here without a coat;

and now you show up with some naked floozy spouting marriage proposals!" He came to stand nose to nose with the other man. "You don't have time for a wife, Stevens. And I don't have time for this nonsense. Where have you been?"

"Following orders, sir. You told me to loosen up." He hugged Maureen. "I did so."

"Well, you've had your fun. Now get dressed and get rid of her! Somehow Carol found out about the Sheti operation. The deal is in severe jeopardy. We have work to do."

Percy shook his head. "It's Christmas. I intend to spend the entire day with Maureen. Your plans for Sheti will simply have to wait."

"Didn't you hear me, Stevens?" Richard's eyes were cold and hard. "I have a terrible hangover and am in no mood for games. Either you do as I say or from this moment you are no longer in my employ. Now get this bitch out of my sight."

"Screw you. Sir." Percy made a fist and socked Richard right on the edge of his elegant jaw. He crumpled to the floor, out cold. "I quit!"

"Thank you for defending me, Percy," Maureen said, kissing him on the cheek. "But are you sure about this? We can't live on my salary."

He patted her hand. "Not to worry, my pet. I have investments of my own, you know." Percival Stevens smiled. "Including a large share of Mr. Palance. Perhaps it's about time someone took *him* over for a change. He's obviously gone clean 'round the bend."

38

"Sean!"
"What?"
"Aye!"
"Over here!"

"Away with the lot of you!" Mike O'Phaelan yelled. "I'm talking to this sorry lout who's been monopolizing my new daughter-in-law to be all afternoon."

Sean hugged Carol, then spun her into the other man's waiting arms. His father whirled her through the crowd of dancing people, a big, proud smile on his face.

As he crossed the room, Sean received so many hearty congratulations that his back was sore by the time he reached the bar. He had a seat, tapping his foot to the music and listening as Percy explained the finer points of snooker to Jack.

Evidently Percival Stevens planned to settle in Denver and open a pub of his very own, with attached snooker parlor. From the way a dedicated eight-ball player like Jack was intently trying to learn the basics of the game, Percy might actually be onto something. Not that he'd have to worry about start-up capital; by the time he finished his other plan of taking over Palance's investment firm, he and Maureen would be set for life.

In some ways, Sean decided, it was what Jack would call a crying shame. Richard wasn't such a bad guy. He'd just chosen the wrong close-knit town in which to ply his nasty cut-throat profession, the wrong woman to put his sleazy moves on, and the wrong man to irritate. He was a victim of fate, in other words.

Then again, maybe he was just shit.

"Let's see," Jack said thoughtfully. "Yellow, green, brown, blue, pink, and black?"

"Correct." Maureen held one of Percy's hands in her lap. In the other, he had a glass of ale. Perhaps he wasn't the happiest man in the room, but he was a close second. "And fifteen reds. You alternate those with the other colors, until all the reds are gone, then pot the ones left in rising order of value. The reds are worth one point, on up to black, which is seven."

"Pot?"

"Pocket," Percy explained. "And a good shooter is called a potter, because he can pot the balls well."

Maureen bumped him with her hip. "Or she."

"You play, my pet?"

"She does," Jack answered for her. "A mean eight-ball player, our Miss Maureen. Taught her myself."

"Then let's have a game!"

"Okay." She stood up. "And just to make it more interesting, why don't we put a bet on it?"

"Money?" he asked. Maureen shook her head. She had a better idea and bent to whisper it in his ear. His eyes went wide, so impressed was he by her creativity. "Good Lord! That will make it interesting!"

Jack chuckled, watching them go hand in hand to the pool tables. He had an itch to play himself, but hadn't quite gotten his arm loosened up. So he sat there, sipping at a beer and watching all the frolic going on around him.

"I was right," he told Sean. "This is turning out to be the best party ever."

Sean nodded his agreement. "I'd better go rescue my fiancée, though. My dad's making her dizzy."

"She was dizzy when she got here," Jack commented. "What's all this about Palance, your friend at Sheti, and some plot to blow him up?"

"My, you have been busy, haven't you?" Sean asked. He shrugged. "It's just a crazy dream she had. Something she ate, probably."

"Or drank. Save any of that eggnog for me?"

Sean turned to look at him, scowling. "And just how—"

"Your grandma told me. I don't suppose *you* would like to tell me what a snowmobile from the Highland Hawk resort is doing parked at the motel down the street?"

Another shrug. "Maybe someone got tired of

the resort's pricey accommodations," Sean suggested.

"Uh-huh." Jack studied his face. "You ever going to tell me what happened last night?"

"You? That's a joke, right?"

"Thought as much," Jack said, disgusted. "Then the least you can do is pour me another beer."

Laughing, Sean did so, then noticed that Carol was now in the evil clutches of his mother and went to save her. It would be tough, but he'd manage. Sean would do anything for Carol. Besides, he'd had a lot of practice saving her lately.

Though he'd never tell Jack, some day he might tell Carol about the call he asked her mother to make last night and the money he'd loaned Frank. But it would be quite some time. Perhaps when he was bouncing grandchildren of his own on his knee. He arrived at the corner table to find the interrogation in full swing.

"So you're an only child?" his mother was asking.

Carol nodded. "Just me."

"Well, I'm sure you can do better."

Sean took a chair between them. His father grinned at him, giving him a knowing wink. "Stop harassing my bride-to-be, Mom," Sean told her. "Don't you think you should wait until I get her to the altar before you start planning our family for us?"

Margret O'Phaelan was unperturbed. "At your age, you can't waste any time."

"Don't worry," Carol said, taking Sean's hand and giving it a squeeze. Her eyes were full of love, and she wasn't one bit scared of the love she could see in his. "I have every intention of using all the precious ticks of my clock to the fullest."

The band struck up a soft, slow ballad, and one of Sean's sisters started to sing. Carol grabbed her future husband's hand and led him out onto the dance floor. The song was sad, but neither of them cried. And when they kissed, no one stopped them. Instead, the whole O'Phaelan brood applauded.

Jack was clapping too, and as he did he noticed his arm was feeling pretty good, so he started looking around for a pigeon. "Now where did Percy and Maureen get to?" he muttered. When the applause died down, he got his answer.

Squeakasqueakasqueakasqueak!

"Damn fool kids! They're gonna wear out their parts!"

Continuing to scan the crowd for a likely pool partner, Jack saw someone farther down the bar who looked familiar. He couldn't put a name with the face, but the way this group wedded and bred, that wasn't too surprising.

He went over to introduce himself. "Howdy! Jack Bensen," he said, extending his hand.

The other man clasped it firmly in his own. "Dr. Louis Powell," he said. His voice was deep and oddly soothing. "Pleased to meet you, Jack."

"I don't believe I've seen you at any of the O'Phaelan get-togethers before. New to the family, are you?"

"No, I'm just an old friend of Sean's."

Jack arched his eyebrows. "Me too. I don't suppose you'd care for a game of eight ball?"

"Don't mind if I do."

They went to the tables. When the game was under way, Jack asked, "What brings you to Tithe, Doc?"

"Oh, a little skiing."

"Two ball, side pocket." Thunk! "Up at Highland Hawk?" Dr. Powell nodded. "Well, always nice to have a vacation, isn't it?"

"Yes. It's been very . . . exhilarating."

"Uh-huh. Four-six combination, both in the corner." *Thunk! Clunk!* "What's your game, Doc?"

"Excuse me?"

Jack chuckled. "In my day, we went to one guy for everything from a broken leg to a bad tooth. Now you're all specialists, aren't you?"

"Oh. Yes, I suppose we are. I'm a research psychologist."

Crack!

"Dang!" Jack exclaimed. "Just look at what I did to the tip of my cue. Your shot, Doc." He went to get another stick, grinning like a fox. "So you're a shrink, huh?"

"I prefer to believe I expand my patients' horizons," the doctor told him, "not shrink them."

"Do tell."

The doctor called and made a shot, warming to both the game and the subject at hand. "I work in dream therapy."

"Is that a fact?" Jack covered his mouth and coughed, hiding a triumphant smile. "It so happens that a friend of mine had a real dickens of a dream last night. Maybe you could figure it out."

"Perhaps. Actually, though, I'm exploring new techniques," he replied vaguely. "Rather hard for the layman to understand. But I'm gaining quite a favorable reputation among my colleagues and have had some astounding successes."

Jack gazed at him. And at last, he remembered another name to go with that familiar face. "I'll just bet you have."

The doctor missed his next shot. Jack promptly ran the table. Then he turned to the other man. "Sorry about that. I practice a lot. I'm basically retired, you know. I play pool, do a bit of placer mining just to keep myself in beer money. And I read," he added. "I read just about everything I can get my hands on. And your work in this technique you call dream *shaping* made mighty fascinating reading. You use timepieces in it somehow, don't you? Isn't that why they nicknamed you Dr. Clock?"

Dr. Powell suddenly paled. "Oh, dear."

Jack looked at Carol and Sean, who were still dancing, wrapped tightly in each other's arms. He smiled. "Don't worry. I love those two kids. Whatever it took to make things turn out this way is fine by me and I'll never tell a soul. But I am curious."

"About what?"

"Isn't it pretty unusual for a world-famous hypnotist like you to make housecalls?"